KILLERS' CANYON

Sandy Crease got his chance to become a private investigator when a senator's brother was murdered in a hotel of his home town. He followed an attractive girl to her family's ranch and clashed with her brother over her possible involvement in murder and robbery. Further probing revealed a connection between the girl and two ruthless drifters, who duped her stepfather over some stolen precious stones. Greed and guilt will lead to three deaths in a canyon before Sandy's first mission is accomplished.

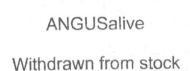

DAVID BINGLEY

◆

KILLERS' CANYON

Complete and Unabridged

LINFORD
Leicester

First published in Great Britain in 1973

First Linford Edition
published 2005

British Library CIP Data

Bingley, David
    Killers' canyon.—Large print ed.—
Linford western library
1. Western stories
2. Large type books
I. Title II. Wigan, Christopher
823.9'14 [F]

ISBN 1–84395–584–9

Published by
F. A. Thorpe (Publishing)
Anstey, Leicestershire

Set by Words & Graphics Ltd.
Anstey, Leicestershire
Printed and bound in Great Britain by
T. J. International Ltd., Padstow, Cornwall

This book is printed on acid-free paper

1

At nine o'clock on a weekday morning in early summer, the thriving town of Drovers' Halt, situated in Raton County, north-east New Mexico territory, was beginning to feel the heat. The main street was full of early morning shoppers. Workers in the saloons and places of late-night entertainment were swabbing out the floors and sidewalks, removing the debris of a previous evening when a barn dance had been held and much liquor had been consumed.

Almost halfway along the street was a double-fronted shop, recently used as offices. Slanting rays of the broiling sun shafted in through the extensive glass of the upper frontage, steadily raising the indoor temperature. Across the front of one office was written in bold gold letters, *Mayor's Parlour. Henry Crease, Mayor.*

The other office had a notice on the door which suggested that it was *to let*, but it was, in fact, occupied. Its occupier was none other than young Sandy Crease, younger son of the mayor.

As the probing rays of the sun fell upon Sandy's half-naked body stretched untidily on a low bed in what would normally have been the front office he began to stir. For a time, he refused to open his lazy blue eyes in the sun's glare. He had been very active at the barn dance and he had consumed quite a quantity of beer in the early hours.

Within fifteen minutes of the start of Sandy's return to consciousness, a man started to walk down the sidewalk of the street with a measured tread. Here and there he acknowledged a passer-by with a word of greeting or a touch of his hat. Nearing the Mayor's Parlour, however, he slowed and frowned.

Town Marshal Dick Crease was the mayor's older son. Dick never liked his mornings after a night of town revelry.

On this particular occasion, he liked it even less because his younger, irresponsible half-brother, Sandy, had made rather a spectacle of himself before the roistering was over.

The Crease family was probably the most influential one in town, but Dick did not trade upon it. He was a tough, relentless, resolute peace officer. His jaw was square, his nose thin and hooked. The tightness of his small mouth and the venomous look which so easily appeared in his grey direct gaze added up to a thorough, unyielding lawman.

At the age of thirty-five he had acquired experience and authority. His marshal's badge was scarcely necessary. Outside the window of the *to let* office he rose on his boot toes and glanced inside, over the glass rendered opaque by paint. He frowned at what he saw within.

He raised his tall dusty black stetson, smoothed his rather greasy auburn hair back off his forehead and sniffed.

Lowering himself, he flapped his black leather vest over his faded squared shirt and studied his reflection mirrored in the window. He unpinned and shifted the position of his star and started to think.

Why should he get worked up about this back-sliding half-brother of his? Their father did nothing but indulge him when he ought to have thrown him out of town long ago to seek his fortune elsewhere.

Sandy was twenty-three now. That meant that twenty-five years had elapsed since Henry's first wife, Dick's mother, had died. To Dick, Sandy was a constant reminder of Henry's re-marriage to a woman totally unsuited to ranch life, or anything at all which called for a woman to rough it.

Unpleasant memories brought him back to the door. He kicked it with the heel of a boot. It shook, being slightly warped in its frame, and the resulting clatter had the effect of suddenly rousing the sleeper.

Sandy sat up, blinking and yawning. 'That you, Dick?'

Dick turned the handle of the door and allowed it to spring open. He stood in the entrance and looked down upon his half-brother with ill-disguised contempt. Meanwhile, Sandy stood up slowly, clapped his hands to the sides of head and massaged his lush fair-to-reddish sideburns as though his head ached. He spied on Dick through his hands. The latter groaned.

'Doggone it, brother, ain't you a sight for a fine summer mornin'? An' don't you make an exhibition of yourself at the dances?'

Sandy groaned. He noted the dryness of his mouth, the reluctance of his eyes to face the light and his older brother's obvious displeasure. He buttoned up his fancy brown shirt and tucked the tails into the waistband of his corduroy trousers.

'Did I do something real bad last night, Dick?'

He was grinning broadly as he spoke

and that had the effect of making the town marshal even less patient than before.

Shrugging in an offhand manner, Dick replied: 'The Mayor will be along inside half an hour. His office will be open to callers. It might be a good thing if you had straightened up all your beddin' an' shifted out of here before someone arrives an' sees the state you've been in!'

Sandy walked a few paces; leaned against the wall. 'My, my, Dick, you sure do have a sensitive disposition, don't you? A few drinks, a few dances an' you're upset! Sometimes I think you're jealous of me, even though it's you the townsfolk look up to all the time! Why don't you relax a little durin' festive occasions an' stop actin' like you have to be careful to keep Pa in office?'

Dick made a half-strangled noise, turned swiftly on his heel and went out, slamming the door behind him. Sandy did not feel particularly fit after his night of roistering. He tried to remember if he had taken a walk with Bonnie

Manton during the proceedings, but he could not remember and presently some vestige of conscience made him go through to the back and sluice himself down under the pump.

★ ★ ★

Mayor Henry Crease made his way along the sidewalk to his parlour some ten minutes later. He had slept well in his semi-permanent room at the Drovers' Hotel, a business which had absorbed some of his excess capital a few years back.

He was sixty years of age and of late he did not look his six feet in height owing to a slight stoop aggravated by approaching obesity and a tailing off of physical exercise. Nevertheless, he looked an imposing figure still with his pink cherubic face and the soft white hair which sprouted out sideways from under his outsize light-coloured stetson.

As he came to the building which housed the parlour, he unconsciously smoothed down his bulk under the well-tailored jacket of his grey suit and shot a quick glance up and down the twin sidewalks, his eyes almost hidden under grey tufted brows.

Some fifty yards or so down the other side of the street was Abel Hall, a small, black-garbed and soberly dressed ex-minister of religion, who was clearly planning on a visit to the parlour with some scheme or another. The mayor frowned slightly, knowing he was in for a protracted and boring discussion on something like keeping the town clean or beautifying it to attract more settlers. Crease yawned and blinked hard.

He stepped towards the twin entrance of the offices. His height enabled him to see that there was no one actually seated in his office waiting for him. That was a relief. He began to wonder if he could smoke a small cigar before the ex-cleric arrived to launch into his suggestions.

Boards creaked under him as he crossed the mayoral parlour and seated himself in a creaking swivel chair which had been re-covered that same year. He pushed back his stetson, hooked gold-rimmed spectacles over his ears and picked up a pencilled sheet of paper which was awaiting him on the desk.

He read: *This town needs a private investigator. Someone other than the regular team of peace officers who could take on private work for influential citizens who want a special service, or well to do visitors passing through. The person is available, and the premises. All that is needed otherwise is about five hundred dollars for starting expenses and the approval of the mayor. What do you think?*

There was no signature at the foot of the note, but none was needed because the writing was immediately identifiable to the mayor, who slumped back in his chair and groaned. Hall's peculiar cough sounded a few yards away up the sidewalk, but young Sandy came in very smoothly from the office next door and was seated in the visitor's chair before Henry had the time to say anything.

Sandy had brushed his grey flat-crowned stetson and done a good job on his brown corduroy jacket which had become soiled the previous night. But for a certain over-brightness of the eyes which a father could not fail to detect Sandy appeared to have made a total recovery from his earlier lethargy.

'Mornin', Pa, well, what do you say to my suggestion? A good one ain't it, especially for a town second only to the county seat in importance?'

The mayor dabbed beads of perspiration off his upper lip with a large white square handkerchief. He looked formidable.

'Son, this is the fourth scheme you've put up for me this year. All the other three failed and they cost me money, as well as loss of face. I will not approve of your becomin' Drovers' Halt's first private investigator, nor will I advance any more money for schemes invented by yourself.

'If you have gambling debts then you'll have to pay for them out of your ordinary allowance, an' that's my last word on the matter. Do I make myself clear?'

Henry's breathing was growing progressively more laboured. At the same time the colour of his face showed that his blood pressure was beginning to play him up. Sandy knew the signs and he realised that he was not likely to make much progress on this occasion. Nevertheless, as he rose cautiously to his feet, he had a few parting words to deliver.

'My Ma wouldn't like your attitude, Pa, an' that's a fact. If I had to ride out to the Circle C an' tell her jest how you've treated me this mornin' you sure as fate would be in the doghouse next time she saw you!'

Henry had it on the tip of his tongue to ask his younger son why he thought he, the mayor, spent so much time in town these days, but he knew that such a response would lead to further heated exchanges and that his blood pressure would not really stand such outbursts.

'Stop tryin' to put yourself up in opposition to your half-brother who is most capable in his job! Leave this office at once an' let me get on with the serious business of runnin' this town. You are becomin' a distinct liability to this town an' my family!'

'Which are more or less the same thing!' Sandy retorted brusquely.

Henry wanted to conclude by asking him to show in Abel Hall, but Sandy was already through the door and was doing just that. The younger son had the distinct advantage of a swift change of attitude and mien and he exercised it on this occasion, leaving the small ex-minister with a rather pleasant impression of the meeting.

Sandy headed for the nearest café to partake of food. He proposed to pay a fairly early visit to the shop owned by Bonnie Manton, and if she was still sleeping off the effects of the dancing and carousing of the previous night, his next choice was a long lazy spell of fishing along a shallow stretch of the nearest creek.

He had no means of knowing at the time that his fishing excursions were about to be severely curtailed.

*   *   *

The Drovers' Hotel was good for the size of the town. It was a three-storey building with some twenty rooms available to the public. Due to the close proximity of the town to the boundaries with Colorado, the Indian Strip and the state of Texas quite a number of visitors guaranteed its continued existence.

One of the rules of the house was that visitors should not be disturbed early in the morning.

Jonas Pullock, the manager, was a conscientious fifty-year-old with strands of grey hair brushed carefully across his balding crown. He started his day's work around eight o'clock and one of his first self-appointed duties was to start and check up on the residents at breakfast in the dining-room.

Some time later, he made a personal visit to the rooms of gentlemen travelling alone who were late to appear and thus it was he who came upon the gentleman in Room Seven, who had already embarked upon the longest sleep of all.

What Pullock saw upon the single bed neatly placed between two rugs in the middle of the room had the effect of profoundly shocking him regardless of the fact that he was very short-sighted and that his spectacles were scarcely adequate.

He stood beside the bed, nervously massaging his shiny grey lapels and raising and lowering his sparse brows. He had never been so shaken since that occasion some fifteen years ago when, as a bank teller, he found himself looking down the business end of a pair of .45 Colts with a masked man behind them.

The man on the bed according to the

hotel register was Mark Hickstead, a native of Trinidad in Colorado. He had been dead for some time because his body had lost a lot of heat since the dagger with the ornate Spanish silver handle had been plunged into his chest.

Pullock started to feel faint. A murder had been committed in his hotel. Or rather in the Crease hotel, which the mayor had been gracious enough to allow him to manage. This was a calamity, indeed. The very undesirable type of happening which the mayor detested. Bad publicity. Bad everything. Pullock knew that there was little he could do. Oddly enough, he did not fear for himself and the possibility that his other clients might be in danger did not seem likely to him.

After making a big effort to pull himself together, he locked the door and personally raced down the street to the Mayor's Parlour, returning with the mayor some five minutes later and still trying to look as though nothing had happened.

Henry Crease was so breathless by the time they both entered the corpse's room that he had to squat on the end of the bed and take it easy for a while. While the mayor absorbed the shock and tried to get control of his faculties, Pullock fed him information.

'A fairly well to do visitor, home town Trinidad, Colorado, Mr. Crease. Name of Hickstead. Mark Hickstead, I think.'

'Hickstead? I ought to know that name,' Crease muttered thickly.

'Almost certainly it must have been a thief disturbed in the night.'

'We'll know more about that when Dick gets here. Does anyone else know about it?'

'Nobody else, sir. I said I thought it was a thief because I know Mr. Hickstead carried a lot of cash with him. And a bag. He had it in the safe for a few hours. Made out of carpeting with draw strings at the top. It seems to be missin'.'

The mayor was thinking that possibly diamonds had been stolen, and that the dead man was probably quite well known in his own area. The town marshal would undoubtedly make a thorough investigation of the killing and the theft, but whether he would manage to apprehend the killer remained to be seen. Inevitably, the hotel and the town would suffer in prestige throughout the south-west, and that was a thing which Henry Crease found very hard to take.

As the boots of his peace officer son resounded on the thin carpet of the stairs, Henry found his mind going back to the words of his younger son, uttered not so very long ago. This sort of investigation might have been better in the hands of a private investigator who to some extent could control the spread of unwanted publicity.

The mayor heaved his bulk off the bed, glanced down at the corpse, still resplendent in bright red pyjamas and skewered with the knife, and awaited the arrival of his older son.

2

Dick Crease was almost as shattered as his father had been, but he had held down peace-keeping jobs in more than one capacity for a number of years and he knew how to go about the preliminaries. First of all, he sent a message to the dining-room for anyone in there to stay at their tables for a while.

The doctor arrived as the breathless manager accompanied by the house-keeper made a tour of the rooms and asked everybody still installed in them to go down below and wait for a message from the town marshal.

The medical man, an old gaunt veteran from the Civil War, had little to do. Hickstead had clearly been killed instantly by a well-timed dagger thrust from the front. It was difficult to estimate the time of death but the doctor thought it might have been in the early hours.

A search of the murder room confirmed that the victim's funds and the bag made of carpeting had been removed. Down below, Dick soon discovered that only two people had vacated their rooms without warning. They were male visitors who had arrived together two days earlier, signed in as Clancy Dune and Roger Brand; place of origin Providence, U.S.A.

A deputy made a search of the vacated rooms and by the time the town marshal had generally put the other guests in the picture and told them what had occurred, his assistant was back again and signalling to assure Dick that he had found nothing incriminating against any of the folks still in residence.

Dick came to the end of his questions and thought things over. His father had long since departed in search of a strong pick-me-up and only the deputy, Raddle, and the hotel manager were still there to back him up.

'Folks, I don't think the killers of this poor man, Mr. Hickstead, are still in this hotel. Nor will they be found around our town. All the same I have to go through the motions of a search and make enquiries, so if any of you could give me a description of the two men who have pulled out, I'd be obliged.'

Dick glanced around him at the cowed folk. After a while, a maiden lady unused to travel plucked up courage.

'Well, Marshal, I saw them both on the stairs, an' I must admit I found them both rather attractive. Not the least like killers. Let me see now. The older one, referred to by his friend as Clan, must have been around thirty-five. He was about your height, nicely built. Rather cool lookin' in a blue-eyed sort of way. His hair was cut short an' he had no beard or moustache.

'The other, the younger one with the guitar, he had brown eyes an' a lot of thick brown hair. He had a long close-trimmed moustache that joined up with the short beard on his chin. He dressed in a black trail outfit an' he wore a sort of steeple type stetson of the same colour. I, er, is that all — I mean is that enough?'

The female's usual timidity had caught up with her. Several of the assembled guests nodded and confirmed what she had said but no one volunteered anything further. They were all too busy weighing up the description with what had happened in Room Seven.

Dick came to his feet. 'Folks, you can come and go now, as you wish. But please don't attempt to leave town till I've spoken to you again at some future time. That's all for now. I think it's fair to say any danger is over.'

The town marshal rose to his feet, beckoned for the deputy to follow him and went out of the building. Men from the undertaker's establishment were already working in the murder room. They waited until most of the guests had dispersed before removing the body from the building to their place of business.

Within five minutes, the wires between Drovers' Halt and the county seat and other towns were humming as the urgent information concerning the killing and the missing guests was relayed.

* * *

Having failed to make contact with Bonnie Manton, one of his girl-friends of the night before, Sandy had carried on to the creek and started to fish. Within a half-hour, he managed to catch three small fish of four to six inches in length and after that his interest started to fade.

He banged off three cylinders of .45 bullets from his Colt at a branch of a tree situated on the other side of the creek. With his right hand he blasted small twigs off the branch nine times out of twelve. His aim with the left hand was not so good, but he did achieve two hits out of six and that made him think that he was improving.

While his gun cooled, he dozed upon the bank and some sort of instinct made him restless after that. He had judged rightly that what was going on in town was far more interesting to all and sundry than the action along the creek.

Deputy Raddle looked thoroughly nonplussed as he conducted his part of the search. Raddle was in his late forties and looked older on account of his straggle of grey drooping moustache and his lined face. He buttonholed Sandy as he came up the street with his rod over his shoulder.

'What's all the excitement about, Rad? You got a rise in pay, or something?'

Sandy had long since hoped to replace him as Dick's deputy, but he did not hold his frustration against the deputy. In fact, on this occasion as always he managed a grin.

'Ain't no laughin' matter, Master Sandy. Last night a man was stabbed to death at the hotel, an' we're askin' around the town for two hombres who didn't occupy their beds last night.'

Sandy's mobile features underwent a change. 'Did they leave without payin' their bill?' he asked, while he marshalled his thoughts.

'No, they didn't. They left coins stacked up on their dressin'-table an' quit the place without makin' any noise durin' the quiet hours. If *I'd* stabbed a man in Room Seven I'd have been out of town so fast my face would have been a blur.'

'What did they look like?'

Raddle gave the descriptions as best he could and even with his chronic lack of skill with words, Sandy recognised two young men who had attended the barn dance the previous evening. In fact, one of them had played a guitar and sung to it while the regular musicians were having a breather.

Sandy had noticed them fairly particularly because at one time Bonnie Manton had showed a whole lot of interest in them. Apparently they had visited her shop and bought things and on at least one occasion they had taken her for a ride out of town.

That they were rivals of his for the attention of Bonnie rather annoyed Sandy, who was in no way put off by her seeming lack of regard for the conventions. He had set his jaw in a firm line when Raddle brought him back to the present with an impatient remark.

'Am I right in thinkin' you've met up with these two hombres, Sandy?'

'Oh, sure, I met up with them all right, along with all the other folks who attended the dance at the barn. Your description was not a bad one, but I can't say I know anything special about them. As sure as fate if they did the killin' they'll have hit the trail by now. What has my brother done about that?'

Raddle wagged a horny finger at him. 'You know your brother's authority don't stretch beyond this town's boundaries, Sandy. He's informed the proper authorities out of town, an' that's all that could be expected of him. Right now, he's tryin' to turn up more information *in* town, so I'll say *adios* if you ain't got anythin' further to add.'

Sandy called him back for devilment and insisted that he should put the fishing rod and fish in the office adjacent to the mayor's parlour. At the same time, Sandy made for the undertaker's and there he was admitted by the head man, Amos Grade, in spite of the painted notice telling strangers to keep out.

Grade thought Henry Crease and his older son had things too much their own way and so from time to time he was indulgent to the younger son who was always permanently kept out of things. Two carpenters were already working on the wood of the coffin and long shavings were building up on the floor of the workshop as Sandy pushed his way though the workers and entered the quieter room where the corpse lay in state on a special bench. Grade was a fat, greyish man in a puckered dark suit and a black stove pipe hat. He was nearing sixty and he had a macabre way with him.

Sandy took off his stetson, nodded towards Grade who was peeling an orange with a fancy silver-handled knife, and stared at the corpse. Grade filled him in on a few details, still consuming the fruit. At an interesting point of time, he held the knife he had been using by the tip and Sandy took it.

'That's what did the damage, young fellow. Nice piece of cutlery, ain't it?'

Sandy screwed up his face in sudden anguish when he realised that the undertaker had been using the murder weapon to cut up his fruit. However, Grade was always an interesting man to converse with and he made an effort not to complain. Five minutes later, and quite a bit more knowledgeable, Sandy hurried out and made his way to the livery at the west end of town.

There, he entered by the main door and whistled in a special fashion. The same whistle came back to him from the loft. Tandy, a teenager with copper-tinted skin who worked casual hours in the building and usually slept in the hay, came down a ladder to speak to him.

At that hour there was no work in hand. The owner was down the street drinking beer and talking about the latest sensation. No one had questioned Tandy as no one knew he had been in the loft.

'You know what they're all talkin' about, Tandy?'

'Sure enough, Sandy. Those two fellers came in after the dance some time an' they were in a hurry to quit town without disturbin' anybody. They argued some as they ran out their horses, an' they finally decided to head for the north. They were ridin' a roan an' a big bay geldin'. Is that what you wanted to know?'

Sandy nodded and grinned and patted the youth on the back. 'Here's two dollars say you can't have my dun saddled and ready to leave town in five minutes, boy.'

Tandy's mouth sagged a little as he weighed up what Sandy intended to do, but he recovered himself, took over the coins and went in search of the dun horse. Sandy was breathless when he returned with sufficient gear to keep him going between towns.

He slotted his Winchester into the saddle scabbard and availed himself of a boost into the saddle. Out in the street, he thanked the youth again.

'Go find my brother, the town marshal, an' tell him what you told me, Tandy. Will you do that for me?'

Tandy rolled his straw hat up his arm and replaced it on his head.

He nodded. 'Jest don't go takin' on too much all alone, Sandy. You hear me?'

Sandy acknowledged and turned the excited dun up the street.

★   ★   ★

29

All the way out of town and on the first few miles north, the young man was calculating how far two riders could get along that trail in the dark hours before dawn. The afternoon was well advanced when he pulled up for a breather on the west side of the trail and poured water into his hat for the dun.

Having slaked his own thirst, he remounted but was slow to pull away. The dun seemed to show a marked interest for the scrub-strewn rocky wilderness on that side, the reason for which was far from obvious. Sandy used the spyglass which he had brought along with him, learning little more.

He had collapsed it and was on the point of riding north again when a voice from the brush and timber off-trail ahead of him arrested his progress.

'Hold it right there, amigo!'

The command was firm enough, and yet it did not seem to have the kind of voice for a road agent. Sandy checked the dun, dropped his reins and slowly hoisted his hands. All the time his heart was thumping, he was telling himself that no one this far out of town could know anything about his self-imposed mission, and that the killers he sought would certainly not have stayed this close to Drovers' Halt merely to hold up a single rider coming north at a later hour.

He licked his lips, and glanced up at his gloved hands.

'That suit you, friend?' he asked calmly.

3

Just as the nape of Sandy's neck began to itch a strange bubbling type of laughter came from the direction of the challenge. Some man was making the noise unseen, and yet he did not show himself.

'If I knew the joke, maybe I could laugh, too, amigo,' Sandy protested.

There was another outburst before the unseen challenger managed to get himself under control and take some of the steam out of the situation. Eventually, the explanation came through.

'I don't have any firearm trained on you, pardner. All I said for you to wait for was 'cause I thought you could use some information an' maybe a cup of coffee. Come on over in the direction of my voice. I can assure you you're in no danger.'

'You're *sure*?'

The hidden man repeated his assurances before Sandy tentatively lowered his arms and finally nudged the dun in the direction of the sounds. Thirty yards up-trail a small grassed park opened out amid the unrewarding foliage and standing in the middle of it was a brightly painted wagon of the type used by travelling salesmen.

Seated on the roof was a small fat gnome of a man with a pink bulbous nose and the ill-assorted features of a clown. On his head was a grey topper. His full red neck was encased in a stiff collar. Lower down, the sleeves of his striped shirt were rolled to the elbows. His knees were doing his chequer-patterned trousers no good at all as he knelt over a series of wooden moulds.

'Sorry I gave you such a shock, friend. Dismount, why don't you, an' help yourself to coffee. You'll find the pot simmerin' over the fire down there. I'll be with you in a minute.'

Sandy nodded. As he dismounted, he read the name on the side of the wagon.

'You must be Wally Bates? You sure did frighten me back there, but I'm glad to make your acquaintance, all the same.'

Bates said a few more words by way of greeting, nipped his bulbous nose with a thumb and fingers liberally coated with wax, and prepared to get down to earth level. Presently, they were taking coffee together, seated side by side on a fallen log.

The pleasantries over and the beverage mostly consumed, Bates grinned afresh. He claimed to be in his middle fifties, but with his full head of greying fair hair and his youthful manner he might have passed for thirty-five.

'I saw your friends go off trail around dawn,' he remarked.

Sandy's mouth opened of its own volition. He spilled the dregs of his coffee over his boots. His consternation did not pass unnoticed.

'Did I say something to upset you, friend?'

Sandy breathed hard. He then whistled to himself, and nodded. 'I was lookin' for a couple of riders who lit out from Drovers' Halt in the early hours, but how could you know that?'

Bates shrugged. 'I didn't. I jest guessed, that was all, after I'd seen you studyin' the terrain on that side of the trail. They found a side-track back there through the sage, an' they went off down there as though they had bad consciences.'

'Can you tell me any more about them?' Sandy asked anxiously.

His heart was thumping hard with excitement. He was prepared to gamble that this casual acquaintance was about to put him on the track of Drovers' Halt's killers. He had the feeling that for once he was going to be thoroughly involved; that on this day of days he was going to go far beyond taking potshots at tin cans and tree branches. He wondered what the outcome would be and whether, after all, this was the sort of assignment best left to big brother Dick.

Bates shook his head. 'Couldn't tell

you much more if I wanted. Dawn is one hour of the day when Wally Bates ain't so friendly. Nor is he wide awake, either. All I can remember is that they thought the trail further north nearer the border might be a little tricky. So they took their chance to cut off to the west. Does that help?'

'And the horses, Wally? Did you get to see them?'

'Jest a glimpse. When I realised where they were cuttin' off trail curiosity made me climb up here on the roof of the wagon. They were ridin' a roan horse an' a bay gelding an' one of them had a guitar slung across his back.'

Sandy offered him a cigar and thanked him warmly. 'Those are the boys I'm lookin' for all right. Only chance made me stop on the trail in this area, though. I didn't have the ghost of an idea they would cut off trail in this region. Incidentally, they are not my friends. They left a dead man back there in town.

'Before I move on again, I'm curious

to know why you're campin' between towns, Wally. Any special reason?'

The little salesman shrugged. 'No mystery there, friend. One of my shaft horses has suffered a sprain. I'm givin' him a rest, a lay off, an' at the same time buildin' up my stock of soap tablets. Anything else I can do for you?'

'Sure. If you run into any posses, tell them what you told me. And say that Sandy Crease from Drovers' Halt went that way.'

Five minutes later, the ill-assorted pair parted with a firm handshake. Sandy's canteen was topped up and he had received a block of soap as a parting gift. More valuable than either, though, to a man so committed was the information he had received.

To say that the lesser track was ill-marked was an understatement. Nevertheless, Sandy took to it and after about ninety minutes the surroundings became a little more luxuriant and less taxing for a through traveller. During the early evening, the orange sun was gradually winning the race towards the west and perceptibly dropping in the sky.

The rider's shoulders slumped and much of the fire had gone out of the dun by the time the track began to loop its way across the southern slope of a bulky hogsback. The heights were up on his right, while to his left the track fell away quite steeply. A man unsaddled at such a place ran the risk of falling around two hundred feet.

Sandy bit his lip and fought to put such considerations out of his mind. He knew he had not much more daylight and he wondered how far ahead the other riders were. On as many as six occasions he had seen definite horse sign, but he was not sufficiently well versed in trail lore to hazard a guess as to how far they were in front of him.

He was never quite clear afterwards which alerted him first, the sharp crack of the fired rifle or the arrival of the bullet which flew up off his saddle horn and narrowly missed his left shoulder.

His stomach muscles tensed. He knew he was under fire from somewhere further up the ridge.

Ahead of him the track was narrow, winding and tortuous. There was no sort of obvious manoeuvre to be made to avoid the attack. A second bullet missed him as he instinctively ducked and reached for the Winchester. Another gun opened up almost at once from another angle, and that made things critical. The dun reacted quite suddenly, rearing up on its hind legs and making further riding well nigh impossible.

Within two or three seconds of the start of the struggle to keep seated, the frightened animal absorbed two bullets. One struck it in the head and the other ripped into its vitals. Either would have killed it. Using the last of its fading strength, it pivoted on its hind legs and fell away sideways.

The rider, clutching his shoulder weapon, felt his stomach lurch as he parted company and started to fall. For a mere second he closed his eyes. In that time, he could well have imagined himself falling for ever. Fortunately, the dying animal did not fall on top of him. He grabbed for what he thought was a stirrup strap but which was, however, a trailing root.

This gradually slid through his gloved hand while the horse crashed past him, loosening earth and sending small shrubs and plants down the slope at the same time.

Sandy had scarcely time to flex his muscles for landing when his boot heel jarred on a rocky shelf. The muscular action threw him forward. As he was facing the cliff side, he pitched in that direction. His senses started to slip as his stetson was swept off and as prickly plants and tree roots buffeted his arms and shoulders.

He slumped and his landing place was much softer than he could possibly have expected.

★ ★ ★

No more than ten minutes had elapsed when his senses started to return. The voices of two men some yards away were muted by the small natural cave into which he had fallen. It had been fashioned the year before when a stunted pine tree had been uprooted in a severe storm. All about him in the semi-gloom were roots and tiny plants which combined to prevent the soil from falling in.

Sandy knew that he was still in some danger, but he had no intention of carrying the fight to his enemies after the tumble he had taken. Somehow, he had retained his hold on the shoulder gun, but in so doing he had strained his wrist. He felt far from his best and his head was unsteady.

He was content to lie low and to know that he had survived the sudden attack of rifles.

'No man could have survived a fall like that, Clan, even if the bullets missed him! Right now, he's probably in that rim rock down there with every bone in his body smashed. So why bother goin' down there to find out? The panic's over. He was alone. He's alone for ever now.'

'All the same, he was right on our tail whether he knew it or not. It jest goes to show that men in our line of business can't ever be too careful. All right, I'll go along with your thinkin', but we'll have to be more careful after this. Let's get back to where we started.'

The voices faded. Sandy was left alone. In the depths of the earth cave, sunset seemed to come much earlier than usual. He stayed where he was, denying himself sustenance. All he did was remove from his person a few burs and attempt to clean up the worst of his scratches and cuts.

In spite of his aches, he slept.

* * *

Dawn was a heightening of the temperature, a noisy invasion of privacy by birds. A badly rolled cigarette afforded the young man some relief as he emerged from his fastness and began to take stock of his surroundings.

His bones ached, his cuts throbbed. The view below the cave was a dizzy drop. The black tail and a twisted hind leg amid rocks reminded him of how the dun had pitched down there. His saddle girths had burst in the fall and the leather saddlery was scattered on the way down.

He spent a whole hour in rounding up his equipment after ascertaining as thoroughly as he could that he was not observed. He felt that the dead horse deserved some sort of shelter. The greater part of its body had fallen between rocks. By hauling on the head harness, he was able to move it a little further. After that, the covering of it was relatively simple. He merely disturbed a quantity of small rocks on the slope above it.

Two hours had elapsed by the time he had contrived and eaten a breakfast of sorts. Standing on the flat rock which had so jarred his heels, he felt like a man on the edge of the world. His father, his brother, Bonnie and the others in town seemed to be on another planet, whereas time itself appeared to have suffered a transformation. That he had merely left town the previous day seemed to have no special significance.

Maybe, after all, he had taken on too much. Maybe he should have stayed in town. What was it that Tandy, the half-breed youth, had said? 'Don't take on too much alone,' or something to that effect.

Sandy's spirits were still low when he started back along the ridge track on foot. By eight o'clock he was looking back over the ground he had covered and trying to calculate what fraction of the return journey he had already accomplished. Clearly, he might be on the way for days. It was not as if he was in a fit and proper condition for a protracted journey on foot. Not after his fall.

He refashioned his crumpled stetson,

pulled it well down over his face and shifted the weighty Winchester from his right hand to his left. Keeping his eyes down so as not to tease himself with the vastnesses ahead, he plodded on again.

He had already learned that his boot heels were in a bad state. Boot heels for a rider can be scuffed and still serve him well, but boot heels for a walker were a different thing altogether. Inevitably, his thoughts went ahead of him and he began to see in his mind's eye the reception he would get when he returned to town in his present sorry condition.

More laughter, more derision, especially from his own. He began to wonder what sort of a life he could fashion for himself if he quitted the security of Drovers' Halt and his family forever. What if he threw in his lot with some sort of travelling outfit and tried to make a living on the trails?

It was easy to speculate, but he was not sure of himself and on this day when all his body ached, apart from the setback to his morale, he had no heart for such considerations. His brooding, however, did send his thoughts back to his friend of the trail side. In the first hour of the afternoon, he raised his Winchester and fired off three shots into the air. An act of desperation, he thought, but to his great surprise, a heavier gun replied almost at once.

Five minutes later, Wally Bates came jogging up on the broad back of a roan shaft horse, a Sharps buffalo gun clasped firmly across his body. He was in his shirt sleeves again and the grey topper looked as if it was glued to the top of his head.

Sandy gasped out: 'Wally!' and sank to his knees.

The small salesman proved himself capable of facing up to the minor crisis. He stripped off Sandy's top clothing and cleaned up one or two gashes on his chest and arms which looked as if they might turn septic. Next, he manoeuvred him on to the horse and supported him on the return journey to the main trail.

Bates had ridden after Sandy purely for something to do, seeing that one of his horses was still not quite ready for wagon pulling. Sandy slept for a few hours on arrival. The stars were out when he managed to rouse himself around the fire and give an account of his setbacks further west.

A full half-hour went by with the wagoner listening well. Before they settled down for the night he asked one or two questions about Sandy's background and appeared to understand.

'You seem to me to be takin' on too much to justify your existence, amigo. Either that, or you're runnin' away from something that bothers you at home.'

Sandy was still brooding over the truth when he slipped away into a deep sleep.

★　★　★

Children, dogs and then grown-ups started to gather about the Bates wagon as it moved slowly up the main street of Drovers' Halt. Wally had fitted a false nose over his real bulbous one and coloured his irregular features with red and white paint. His efforts drew the usual responses, but almost everyone knew Sandy Crease and his pale face and strapped right wrist told of a story worth hearing. Many people followed the wagon. They seemed surprised when it halted outside the peace office rather than in the usual square.

Very speedily, a ring of sightseers hemmed the wagon and team beside the sidewalk. Dick Crease and his father stepped out from the marshal's office with a quietly deliberate tread. They acknowledged their kin as Wally handed him down, but already, in spite of the mayor's presence, men were sniggering about the second son's latest escapade.

Marshal Crease forced a grin which sat uneasily on his hard feaures. 'Good of you to bring in this young fellow, Mister Bates, seein' as how he's lost his horse somewheres. We're obliged to you, the mayor and me.'

Neither of the older Creases made any attempt to step forward and help the passenger, but Bates was quick to get down and assist him into the office. The mayor exchanged a few sallies with men he considered worthies in the crowd. He then followed the marshal into the office and saw his younger son swaying on his feet in front of the scarred desk.

'I've got information for you, marshal,' Sandy announced in a strained voice.

Dick moved around him and planted a hip on the edge of the desk.

He replied: 'Brother, I've got news for you. You don't shape up too well on foot!'

In spite of his weakness, Sandy coloured up. Dick was no more than a yard away and the fixed grin on his face seemed to do something to him.

Suddenly he tensed himself and swung with his left hand. A fist landed high on the marshal's head and toppled him from his perch over the far side of the desk.

Roaring with anger, Dick picked himself up. Bates, who had been hovering near the window, moved nearer before the mayor could interfere. Sticking a chair behind Sandy's knees, the salesman pushed him into it.

'What's the matter with you Creases?' the small man bellowed angrily. 'There's no wonder this young fellow's quit town and tried to get himself killed somewhere else! I'd run away from the pair of you myself!'

Dick, by this time, had recovered his feet and was standing in a menacing pose in front of his seated brother.

'He's been doin' your sort of work, marshal, chasin' killers! Will you take control of yourself while he tries to tell you what happened?'

This time the apparent gravity of the situation penetrated to the mayor. He stepped in front of Dick and advised him to go up the street and take a beer.

'All right, Mr. Bates, I'll take over now. Why don't you go on out there an' entertain the townsfolk with your antics or something?'

'I'll do that, mayor, but see you treat him gently is all. He has a lot to say to you.'

Sandy murmured his thanks through cracked lips as Bates slipped out of the office and received an ovation.

4

In spite of recent festivities during which many of the local population had overspent, Wally Bates's clowning and salesmanship were well received. In an hour, late in the afternoon, he turned over enough money to keep him comfortably on the road or in town for a week or ten days.

It was then that he began to regale the crowds with tit-bits which he had learned from Sandy on the return journey. He soon had a clear impression of the general assessment of the youngest Crease and he set about changing the young man's image in his own subtle fashion.

The time moved along, turning afternoon into evening. Many people went home or turned to other forms of entertainment. Strolling sightseers who had no taste for saloons halted in groups near the square and bought small articles in order to be in touch with Bates and to ask him questions.

Bonnie Manton was one of those who came along in the early evening, having already heard many rumours about Sandy's spectacular return to town on the box of the travelling man's wagon. She was a tall and shapely girl with sufficient poise to be taken for more than her twenty-three years.

On this occasion she was wearing a low-cut bottle-green dress which clung to her waist and billowed out lower down over the hips. A Mexican poncho with a narrow aperture hid most of what the gown revealed.

'Mr. Bates, I'd like half a dozen blocks of that nicely scented soap you always carry. Do you have that much?'

'Why for certain sure, miss. I *always* have plenty, an' when I haven't I can always conjure some out of the air for a complexion like yours!'

Bates dipped down into the bowels of his vehicle to find extra stock. Bonnie blushed. She was not a native of the town, although most of the people accepted her readily enough. Her prettiness attracted the men and her seeming lack of restraint on occasion made some of the more strait-laced ladies a little doubtful of her.

While Bates was down out of sight, some men who normally avoided looking at Bonnie chose this occasion to get an eyeful. His talk had made them brave their wives' disapproval.

Compared with the handful of eligible girls of the town, Bonnie was quite an attractive proposition. She had a long swan-like neck which endeared her to many. Her black hair was long and severely drawn back from a broad forehead on either side of a central parting. Sometimes she rolled the bulk of it into a bun. On this occasion it was tied back at the nape of her neck in a green ribbon. She coyly flashed her green eyes to right and to left. Women stared at their men as they took the hint and looked away.

Finally, Bates appeared with the parcel of soap already wrapped.

'Will there be anything else, miss?'

'Er, no, nothing else, Mr. Bates. I'd like to ask if Sandy Crease really was knocked about like the folks are saying, though.'

'He was severely knocked about all right, miss. Almost shot to death. Are you a friend of his?'

Bonnie blinked and then laughed easily. 'I believe I could say that. He was one of several young men who pursued me quite a lot at the last dance. Has he, will he have retired for the day, would you say?'

Bates grinned. 'That's something you'll have to find out for yourself, miss. I can tell you he's tired as well as hurt. But he did take a swipe at his brother, the marshal, not very long after he hit town. You'll have to wait and see, won't you?'

The little salesman ogled the girl as she stepped away from the wagon and retraced her steps. Because of his greasepaint he was permitted to get away with such a liberty. It soon became clear that Bonnie was aware of his protracted interest because her warm laughter floated back up the street with its special sort of enchantment.

★ ★ ★

Two hours later, the light began to fade. By that time, Bonnie was back in the apartment over the top of her shop. Two lamps were lighted in the sitting-room, and another woman, Marie McClore, was there keeping Bonnie company.

Marie McClore was a war widow. She worked for Bonnie both as a needlewoman and as a shop assistant, and as Bonnie frequently liked a change, Marie came in for a lot of the work. On this particular evening, Marie was stiching tiny costumes for marionette figures made by Bonnie. Apart from being a shopkeeper, Bonnie had a talent for wood carving which she had picked up as a young girl from her father.

Bonnie sat back in a low chair and worked the strings of the puppets, which were going to be Mexican dancers. As she did so, she hummed a staccato Spanish dance melody to herself and her feet were going to the beat.

The conversation became spasmodic after a time. Bonnie tired of her assistant's company, but she was reluctant to tell her to go home. Marie yawned, moved her spectacles further up her nose and squinted more closely at her needlework. The younger woman shifted the nearer of the two lamps so that she could see better.

Marie raised her brows, so that her forehead wrinkles were deepened. She already had an inkling to go home, but curiosity was keeping her at her work.

'Bonnie, you've been around Drovers' Halt for quite a time now. I sometimes wonder if you're thinkin' of settlin' down? After all, you're not short of admirers, are you? Do you have a favourite among all those young men who want to dance with you?'

Bonnie pouted and raised her delicately arched brows.

'If you want to know the truth, I'm feelin' particularly restless this week, Marie, an' that last dance hasn't made me feel any more settled. Now, why don't you get yourself off home an' stop worryin' about me? Those costumes can be finished tomorrow.'

Marie shrugged and smiled wanly. While she was making up her mind what to say by way of reply, a man's footsteps were heard mounting the outside staircase to the apartment. The older woman took off her glasses, smiling broadly.

Seconds later, Sandy Crease knocked on the glass panel of the door and admitted himself, hat in hand. 'Hope I'm not interruptin' anything, ladies. This is jest a social call. Wondered how you were makin' out seein' I've been out of town for a while.'

The women exchanged mute glances. Marie saw by Bonnie's expression that she was not expected to stay. Most young women of Bonnie's age would have wanted a companion on an occasion like this, but not Miss Bonnie. She had very advanced ideas for her time, and Marie knew better than to go against her wishes. Besides, the young gentleman on this occasion was the son of the first townsman, and that had to mean something. Maybe there was something special between the two of them, after all.

Sandy discarded his hat and opened the outer door for Marie to leave. He then seated himself in the chair vacated by her, and received a glass of wine from a cut glass decanter. In handing it to him, Bonnie sniffed.

'My, my, the doc sure has been dosin' you up, boy. You smell like a surgery you got so much liniment on you.'

The girl seated herself opposite and raised her glass to him.

'Tell me about your trip, won't you?'

Sandy shrugged and really seemed as if he wanted to keep it to himself. He looked for somewhere to put his eyes while he talked about his exploits. Bit by bit, he laid his adventures on the line and Bonnie listened well.

All the time he was talking, Sandy was going over the little ornaments, bits of lace, ladies' small accessories and so on scattered over the table. He was well launched on the part of his narrative relative to the return journey when something extremely unusual caught his eye and held his interest.

Two round smooth red stones had been fashioned into ear-rings of sorts. Each one had been provided with a small net made out of gold-coloured silk thread. Sandy pawed them about delicately with his left hand and flashed Bonnie a look of mute enquiry. She gave him a coy look, welcoming his interest but offering no information.

'Bonnie, you've heard all about how this poor man, Hickstead, was stabbed in the hotel an' yet you don't offer any sort of comment. Aren't you shocked by the event?'

The sudden questioning startled her. The look in her eyes showed that she was weighing her answer.

'I'm sorry, of course. But I don't know the man an' no harm has come to me. The west is a violent place and this sort of things goes on. How can I feel strongly for a man I never knew?'

Bonnie was asking questions in her turn. She seemed at a loss to answer adequately. Sandy reflected that it was difficult to really know her and he changed his line of questioning.

'Am I right in thinkin' these are ear-rings, fashioned for special occasions?'

Sandy picked them up, one in each hand. Bonnie raised one brow, a habit she had when she wanted to show caprice.

'Why, is there some young woman you want to buy them for?'

The visitor yawned. 'It wouldn't interest you if I had, would it?' he remarked tartly. 'Now, do me a favour. Put them on before I go.'

Bonnie already knew what they would do for her as she had made the holding nets herself. She rose gracefully to her feet, crouched in front of a tall mirror and carefully inserted her right ear into one of the small meshed bags. Unable to resist the chance, Sandy moved around to her and clumsily assisted the second operation with his left hand.

He stood back and regarded her closely.

'Glory be,' he murmured, 'they certainly do a lot for you, Bonnie. And you have a happy knack of fashionin' and wearin' such baubles.'

A few notes of laughter trilled out of the back of her throat. She tossed her head this way and that. In the lamplight, even though the stones were uncut, the effect was almost uncanny. Sandy lunged at her, hoping to clutch her to him and steal a kiss, but she easily dodged his bandaged right hand

and merely brushed his cheek with her lips as she went away from him.

A sudden thought made him refrain from pursuing her.

'Those stones might be valuable. Where did you get them from?'

Bonnie danced around the room until she tired of the ploy. She then slipped into a chair, removed the baubles and also took off her poncho. Wrapping the blanket garment around her legs, she sat down in an armchair. Her face went so blank that her visitor might never have been there.

'I asked you a question a moment ago,' he prompted gently.

'So you did,' the girl replied with a languid sigh. 'An admirer gave them to me. Pushed them through the door in an envelope. Kind of generous, wasn't he, especially if they're worth a lot of money?'

'Was it one admirer, or two, Bonnie?' Sandy persisted.

Suddenly her eyes flashed fire. 'Now see here, Sandy Crease, your folks may own most of this town, but they don't own me. Nobody owns Bonnie Manton an' that's a fact. You're asking too many questions an' you're embarrassin' me at this hour, so I'll have to ask you to leave!'

Sandy knew her quick bouts of temper and he hoped that she would become calm again and encourage him to stay longer, but this time his luck was out. Clearly, she wanted rid of him and he had no option but to collect his hat and make for the door.

'Thanks for the wine,' he murmured before leaving.

'That's quite all right, Sandy. Thank you for callin'. I'm glad you weren't hurt too badly.'

He stepped through the door and started down the stairs, hoping against hope that he would think of something startlingly original to say before she closed the door above. A thought occurred to him.

'Bonnie, you ought to get some expert to cut those stones for you, then they'd really be worth something! They'd be more attractive, too!'

Her head appeared momentarily in the door opening.

'You have a good idea there, Sandy. I might jest do that. Adios, an' to bed with you!'

She waved and withdrew. Sandy went slowly down the rest of the steps and halted at the bottom. Consorting with Bonnie was always exciting, he found, even when she was in an awkward mood. As he paused and thought over their exchanges, and reflected upon the business of the two uncut stones, her rich melodious laughter penetrated down to him from the apartment.

Something had moved her greatly, but it was hard to tell what.

5

Senator Jacob S. Hickstead, of Trinidad, Colorado, hit the town of Drovers' Halt the morning after Sandy Crease had returned from his skirmish with the gunmen further west. The best known senator in the state to the north of New Mexico territory had been away from his home town at the time of his brother's murder and, because of that, he was out of touch with the arrangements for the burial of the unfortunate victim.

When the wires started to hum, the senator was over the border to the east of New Mexico, looking into the development and conditions of small communities in the Indian Strip. Very few settlements had the telegraph wires through in that territory and so he started the journey west to the location of his brother's demise handicapped by a late start.

A specially appointed stagecoach brought him the last few miles into town. It had been sent along by the county authorities in Placer City, located well to the south. Hickstead's actual arrival was also unfortunate because it almost coincided with the time of the burial in the local cemetery.

In fact, when the celebrated visitor stepped down from the coach and started to kick up the dust there was no one about to see to his bags, or to console him for his loss.

The shotgun guard came down off the box and personally went to find someone to attend to the passenger's needs. Eventually, he found a barman sleeping off his late hours on top of his long bar and the information came out that the funeral was already in progress at Boot Hill.

'Well, why in tarnation couldn't the fools wait until I got here?' the new arrival bellowed.

The guard looked cowed and shied away towards the driver who wondered whether he ought to pull away and see to the needs of his team, as was customary, or hold on and try and be of more assistance. The barman, baggy-eyed and blue-chinned, cleared his throat.

'Maybe they didn't know you were so close, mister. Maybe the message never got as far as town.'

Hickstead raised his two carpet bags as if he was a weight-lifter. He swung them above his head, banged them together and dropped them in the dust again. Tales of his furies had circulated throughout the south-west ever since he had made the United States senate.

He was a bulky man with a bull horn voice. Sixty arduous years had given him a slight stoop and his sagging cheeks looked to be weighed down by his thick grey sideburns. After the long journey west, his black suit was creased and dusty and the light cloak which he had slung over one shoulder did nothing to enhance his appearance.

The western sun had rendered his

complexion the colour of copper almost and his grey myopic eyes appeared to have deliberately receded under his formidable brows. On his head, hiding the steel-grey hair, was a round black hat finished in silk. This, he twisted about in his impatience as though it fitted to his head by a screw thread.

'Hell an' tarnation, the Indian Strip where I've jest come from is a far better place to be dumped down in than — than Drovers' Halt, so help me. You, you man! There's five dollars for you if you can find a buckboard or something an' take me up to Boot Hill before it's too late! You hear me? An' you other two, off with you! See to the horses an' report back to me later! Git goin'!'

The bull horn voice echoed up and down the street and the few people who had not taken time out to go and watch the stylish funeral arranged by the mayor were treated to a preview of the difficulties to come.

Carrying his own bags, the senator moved to the nearest sidewalk and seated himself. He gave himself a pinch of snuff from a silver box and delicately sniffed it up, half into each of his nostrils. Presently, he sneezed, and while he was still working on the lower part of his face with a big blue handkerchief a small battered-looking buckboard came down from the nearest intersection with a short-legged pinto in the shafts.

'Sure as fate I don't know who this belongs to, but seeing as how you're in such an all-fired hurry to get to the plantin', sir, I don't suppose anybody will mind you borrowin' it!'

The blue-chinned barman who was motivated by the offer of ready cash, hoisted the two bags onto the buckboard and coaxed the traveller to mount up on the box. Hickstead looked as though he was about to argue some more, but he thought better of it and instead, clambered up beside the makeshift driver and glared at the pinto's rump.

The painted horse went off at a

modest pace, and two thoroughfares were crossed before the late arrival began to leave town and go up the high ground towards the cemetery. Unfortunately, just as the whitewashed walls of the burial ground came into sight, the first of the people who had attended the service started to come away.

Among their number were those who had only attended out of boredom in other matters and they cascaded around the buckboard thoroughly disquieting the pinto which lashed out at the following conveyance with its hind legs.

'Will you look what you're doin' before you have us capsized?'

Several people, slow to put on their hats, glared at the incongruous figure of the man who had arrived too late, wondering who it was that he was tongue-lashing. Clearly, it was not the driver of the buckboard, so it had to be themselves.

'For your information, stranger, this is neither the time nor the place for a show of bad manners. Only an intruder would arrive at this time, jest when folks are hastenin' away from the service!'

The man in question would have said more but he happened as he spoke to look intently into Hickstead's face and something in the malevolent expression cut short his words.

'Stop the horse!'

Blinking hard, the barman did as he was told. He got down off the box, offered to steady his passenger on the way down and was ignored. Presently, Hickstead was standing beside him, hands on hips and looking for a new target for his wrath. When the barman made no attempt to go away again, the senator turned a sharp glare upon him and was surprised when he did not flinch.

'It wasn't my fault the service was over before we got here, sir. I did my best. In my own free time, too!'

The copper coloured skin turned a new tinge, almost maroon for a moment or two. And then he gave in, parting with a five dollar bill which he had thought to return to his bill-fold.

'Leave the buckboard now and show me to the grave,' Hickstead instructed, clicking his dentures with his tongue.

The barman shrugged. 'All you have to do is go the other way to all these people an' you'll find it easily enough. Me, I've got to get back, otherwise I might find myself arrested as a horse thief by some peace officer with too little to do!'

Hickstead found himself nodding and agreeing with the barman's sentiments. They parted company at that point and Hickstead forced his way through a narrow gate against the weight of several people. Some glared, others muttered. He ignored them all. As soon as his boots were upon one of the trimmed footpaths he began to move faster. To right and to left, those who were coming away gave ground.

Presently, he came out into the trampled area where the grave actually was. Some ten or twelve people were still there, but they had stepped back from the grave and were talking quietly among themselves. The parson, hair blowing in a light breeze, went off with his hands behind him, making a lone tour of the burial area.

Hickstead removed his round hat, unnoticed for a time, and stepped close to the mound which had just been filled in. He squinted down at the newly turned earth, and his expression softened for the first time since he had arrived. He knelt and for a while prayed. And then he was up again and examining the floral tributes.

He cleared his throat. 'Tell me, does the mayor happen to be here?'

Henry Crease detached himself from his second wife, who had come into town specially for the occasion. Leaving her to the care of Dick, he stepped forward, hat in hand, having just guessed the latecomer's identity.

'You must be Senator Hickstead, the senator, from Trinidad in Colorado. I'm glad to know you, sir, even though this is a sad thing which brings us together. As you can see, we've done what we could for your late lamented brother. The whole of our town shares the sorrow which his untimely death must have brought to you.'

Hickstead admitted his identity. His manner showed that he was in no mood to be introduced to the mayor's wife, or anyone else at that particular time. He thanked the mayor brusquely for his condolences and then quietly started to reassert himself.

'Mayor, your floral tributes do you credit, but your timin' was all out. Why couldn't you have waited a while longer to see how and when I was likely to arrive here?'

'Er, excuse me a minute, senator?'

Sensing the atmosphere and the type of exchanges he was in for, Henry wisely turned his back for a moment or two on his distinguished visitor and showed by covert gestures that he wanted his wife, his son and the others to quit the burial ground with as little fuss as possible and leave the senator in his hands.

They took the hint quite quickly, and to cover their smooth withdrawal, the mayor started to explain loudly and in much detail about the slight breakdown in effective communications between his town and the country seat. He was still busy two minutes later when Hickstead peered beyond him and saw that they were alone.

'I've been here long enough, Crease. With your permission, I'd like to withdraw.'

Crease headed the pair of them away from the burial plot with a last backward glance of pure reverence at the mound and the flowers which capped it. He was fully aware now that his companion was one of the most formidable politicians in the south-west and he intended to make the most of this whole unfortunate incident.

The journey down into town was in a buggy. Halfway back again, Hickstead broke a respectful silence by starting to make known his immediate wants.

'When we get back into that — that main street of yours, I want to be installed in the hotel, in the same room as my brother occupied when he was murdered.'

Although he was clearly upset, the senator did not flinch when he used the ugly word. Mayor Crease opened his mouth to ask if that was a wise thing to do, but he was not given the time to open up about it.

'Give me half an hour an' then the interviews can start. You'll know all the folks I should talk to, so they won't keep me waitin' unduly if you handle that end of the business. You know what I mean?'

The mayor shrugged and replied in the negative.

'I want to be put in touch with everyone in authority in this town. All peace officers. Anyone who can tell me anything at all about my brother's stay here and the circumstances which led up to his death.'

Crease, a formidable man upon his own territory up until this time, began to quake inwardly. At first he had thought that Hickstead's visit might be of benefit to Drovers' Halt, but now he was not so sure.

'I have interests in the hotel. You can have the same room as your brother, sir. May I ask if you were intendin' to visit our town, other than for the funeral?'

'I was, indeed, Mayor Crease. At the present moment I am preparin' notes for speeches on the under-developed south-west. Speeches in the Senate, you understand, and also the notes will be used for a book about territories which have not yet attained statehood.

'I might say that the Indian territory has interested me greatly, whereas Raton County, New Mexico territory so far has left me feelin' kind of flat. Maybe the folks of this town will improve my thoughts on the matter.'

★   ★   ★

Hickstead spent his half-hour of grace in cleaning himself up and disposing of a light lunch brought in from the nearest café. He had scarcely emptied his mouth when the mayor knocked and entered, hoping to ask who should be the first interviewee. Henry Crease was at once put down in a chair and became the first victim.

The cross-examination was formidable. Some of it was occasioned by a natural and determined curiosity stemming from the murder and the rest was prompted by the politician's natural talent for finding out about places and people.

Unfortunately, as Dick followed and then the manager of the hotel, Hickstead's doubts about town security began to increase. He was a hard man to argue with and within ninety minutes it was being whispered up and down the main street that he was dissatisfied and that he had the dignitaries in a state of mounting distress.

From time to time, in an effort to say

something concrete in answer to criticisms, men mentioned the efforts of young Sandy, and so it was that five minutes after his late return from the fishing creek he found himself in Hickstead's presence.

'I'm Hickstead, senator, from Trinidad. Take a seat, young fellow and make yourself at ease. Rumour around here has it that you yourself took more positive action than anyone else in town following the murder of my brother.'

A bottle of whisky was pushed towards him, also a cigar, and as the senator was not impatient to start the talk, Sandy found himself warming to the irascible old man who primed himself continually with liquor, nicotine and snuff. All the time his hands were empty, Hickstead toyed with the murder weapon as though personal contact with it would tell him what he most needed to know.

'You'll allow my brother, the marshal, has no jurisdiction out of town, senator. I elected to ride out alone because I was angry with my folks. I wanted to set myself up as a private investigator, but I couldn't get the backin'. Maybe I was wrong.'

Hickstead objected to his summing up of himself and insisted that he got on with the story and stopped trying to whitewash his folks. Every now and then, Hickstead asked a question. There was a pause after some twenty minutes, although it was clear that the politician's mind was still busy with some scheme.

'If I were to give you capital to start you up as a private investigator would you follow the cold trail of my brother's killers?'

Sandy blinked, raised his brows and instantly nodded. 'There's one source of information in this town not known to the peace office. I think I might jest get a lead on where those two jaspers are headed, 'cause they won't any longer be in the place where they fired on me.'

Hickstead allowed him to run on for

a few minutes. Satisfied, the senator then butted in. 'Five hundred dollars will be made available to you tomorrow. Buy another horse an' get started right away. I want those hombres tracked down. Why anyone would want to kill Mark for a bag full of uncut commercial diamonds, rubies an' sapphires I'll never know, unless they were basically the murderin' kind.

'I'll telegraph all the main banks in the towns within a radius of fifty miles from here. That way you'll have backin' an' funds wherever you go. Me, I'll hang on here for a while an' start writin' my book. But you must send me a message over the wires every so often an' let me know how things are workin' out. That scheme suit you, son?'

Sandy shot to his feet grinning and full of enthusiasm. He offered his sprained hand to be shaken and did not wince when Hickstead's pressure gave him pain.

'I'll be up shortly after dawn, Mr. Hickstead, an' I won't be in town for very long after breakfast time. Good day to you now, an' I hope you have a lot of success with your book.'

Hickstead grinned, showing stained teeth.

'It always makes me feel good to see a man of action ready to take off. I'll be up early enough to see you before you go.'

6

Sandy was the first customer in his regular café for breakfast. Before he had finished eating, the senator joined him. After that, they went along together and looked over some horses before the semi-retired liveryman (interviewed by the senator earlier) had the time to dress properly or to eat his breakfast.

The young man found himself coming away with a spritely skewbald and the necessary horse jewellery to go with it. Together, they entered the peace office where Dick had to make a statement about what was happening around the county in regard to the protracted search for the elusive killers.

No less than three posses from other places had been busy, but none of the deputised men had so much as laid eyes on the two wanted men. Other messages from over the borders to the north and east reported no successes. Hickstead then led the way to the bank, almost out-stripping his latest protégé with his long impatient strides.

The senator made arrangements for funds for Sandy and made sure that he had plenty of notes for use on his trip. It was only when they were out on the street that the old politician calmed down a little and stopped trying to organise things.

'You said you had a source of information in town. Want me to come along with you?'

For the first time, Sandy asserted himself. 'No, Mr. Hickstead, I don't want you with me. We'll part here an' if there's anything special to tell you I'll leave a message on the way out. So I'll jest shake your hand an' be on my way, if that's all right with you.'

Hickstead approved after the briefest of hesitations. He went off down the sidewalk while Sandy was mounting up. Presently, he came back again and offered the murder weapon, handle first. 'If the jaspers offer fight, don't do yourself harm by tryin' to take 'em alive, young fellow.'

The old man nodded and when he moved off this time, he did not look back. Sandy put the dagger in a saddle pocket and urged the skewbald in the direction of Bonnie's shop.

Right from that moment he knew that it was going to be a long job.

* * *

Marie McClore was sweeping the sidewalk in front of the shop and she greeted him warmly, showing curiosity. Bonnie was not about, and she was not in her bed. Sandy wondered if she had slipped away while he had been buying the horse, or chatting at the bank, but Marie soon settled his mind on that score.

Bonnie had left town the previous afternoon. No one was supposed to know where she had gone. Sandy began to look desperately anxious. Had not

Marie thought that he was in love with her, he would have found it hard to get further information from the hired woman.

Grudgingly, Marie decided to give him a lead as he finished off the outdoor work for her. Inside the shop, with just the counter between them he heard what he most wanted to know.

'She's a girl of good family. Her folks own a ranch out Conchas Creek way. That's to the south-west. She didn't tell me in so many words that she was goin' home, mark you, nor did she say how long she would be away for, but one or two little hints in the last day or two make me think that's where she's gone. If you're plannin' on followin' her, you're not to tell her I told you where to look. Is that understood?'

Sandy nodded, grinned and squeezed her hand. He wanted to tell Marie that there was more behind his enquiries than she thought, but he did not dare do that in case something went wrong at the outset. He angled about for a little more information and when he had ascertained that she had taken the ruby ear-rings with her he was ready to go.

His only other stop was at the office by the mayor's parlour. There, he wrote a short note for his father, asking him to explain to his mother that he would be out of town on business for a while. Another short note for the senator hinted that he might be on his way to Conchas Creek. A third missive was to thank Wally Bates for his help.

Five minutes later, he was clear of town. He was starting on what might be a very long journey, and his direction was a gamble because he thought that Bonnie was more interested in the two killers than she allowed people to think. She might even be following them because of the two red stones which so far were uncut. Or maybe it was just their style which attracted her.

As the shoes of the skewbald stirred up the dust under him, he could not help reflecting that although he knew

Bonnie as well as any young man in town he did not really know her at all.

★　★　★

Three days riding brought him into Conchas Creek. It was the most westerly town in Raton County, rather isolated from other settlements and built upon noticeably higher ground rising into the eastern plateaux of the Rocky Mountains.

His arrival was on the right side of noon and he was therefore in a position to ask questions in the bars before the regulars went away to their jobs or began their siestas. He was anxious to begin his search at once, and something he had brought with him helped to cut down on the questions which at times could seem endless. His aid, on this occasion, was a small photograph of Bonnie which he had misappropriated at an earlier date.

A Mexican with a knowing look in his eye recognised her in the third *cantina* that he visited.

'You mean you don't know where to locate this *senorita*?'

Sandy flashed a grin. 'You tell me, then I'll know.'

'This is the daughter of the Manton spread, the Box M. You must be one of the reasons why she is away from home so much. I wish you luck, *senor*.'

Sandy thanked his informer and asked the way to the spread. He took note of the directions, prowled around for a while in case the girl was still in town and finally started the skewbald on its second journey of the day.

The Box M was quite an extensive ranch. He found his way onto Manton territory without exciting too much curiosity and he was just about to pull out his spyglass for a close look at the cluster of home buildings when someone who had sneaked up on him from the back of the timber stand clicked a gun at his back and requested him to dismount.

Sandy stiffened, but he only hesitated

for a short while before getting out of the saddle with his hands well clear of weapons. He raised his arms, still holding the glass in one hand. The idea of using it as a weapon had occurred to him, but the swarthy Box M cowpuncher who had taken exception to his scrutiny decided to take him along to the Boss without delay and that made the risky move against the gun quite unnecessary.

Ten minutes later, Sandy hitched the skewbald to the rail in front of the green-shuttered ranch building and leaned on the gallery rail while the suspicious cowpuncher called the top man out of the house.

His measured tread preceded him. Sandy studied him as he came out through the front door, blinking his eyes in the sunlight. Clearly, this was Bonnie's brother and he did not look to be in favour of strangers. Sandy wondered why.

'Good day to you, Mr. Manton, I'm a friend of Bonnie's. Your man there took

91

exception to me squintin' at the house through my glass. I'm sorry if I showed too much curiosity.'

Manton nodded to the man and dismissed him. Jeff Manton was six feet in height and well proportioned for his size. He had a set, sober, almost troubled expression on his deep-tanned face. At either side of the big dun side-rolled stetson, a scattering of silver hair showed among the black ones. His grey eyes did not sparkle like Bonnie's. They lacked lustre.

Stroking the fawn shirt down his ample chest, the rancher, who was around thirty-two years of age, advanced the conversation.

'Bonnie ain't here an' she's not expected. Do you mind tellin' me who you are an' why you're here?'

'Could we talk inside, Mr. Manton?'

Reluctantly, the young rancher gave his permission, heading his visitor into the house. The dining-room and parlour were on the right of the door. The two men ended up sitting on either side of the dining-room table with their hats in their hands.

'I'm Sandy Crease. I come from Drovers' Halt in the north of the county. That's where I've known Bonnie. She has a shop which sells souvenirs and things that women like to buy. Like those carved models you have on the mantelpiece.'

Sandy thought he was making out a good case for knowing Bonnie, but this taciturn brother of hers either didn't want to know about it or he was keen to see the back of his visitor.

'Go on, I'm listenin'.'

'Bonnie left the shop a day or two ago in something of a hurry. I followed her for several reasons. There was a murder in our town. The brother of a Colorado senator was stabbed to death in our main hotel. The two men who killed him have gotten clean away so far. They took with them a bag of stones, diamonds, rubies and so on.

'Bonnie received two red stones from an admirer before she left. I think one of those killers gave them to her.'

Holding his stetson like a boomerang, Manton pointed it at his visitor. 'Are you suggestin' that my sister is the associate of thieves an' murderers?'

'I'm not tryin' to blacken her character. She may be in possession of stolen property, for a start. Secondly, if she associates with these men again, innocently, she could be in some danger. Don't you see that?'

Manton lowered his hat. He looked puzzled and irritated. 'Are you suggestin' that two murderers are hidin' away on my territory, Crease? Because if you are, I can assure you they aren't. They wouldn't get any nearer to this ranch house than you did before one or other of my boys spotted them an' then they'd be rounded up. Satisfied?'

Sandy looked this way and that. He wondered if there was any real affection between this hard-faced brother and the girl he had been looking for. While he hesitated, the rancher stood up.

'My sister ain't here. An' what's more she's — she's resourceful. She wouldn't go associatin' with killers an' thieves unless it suited her purpose. You get me? She ain't likely to take any harm, but she ain't here. There's no one here who didn't ought to be, so if that's all you've got to talk about I'd like to ask you to leave.'

Manton circled the room, knocking chairs aside with his legs. At the door which led through to the rear part of the house he paused. Throwing it open, he called through it. A plump greying Mexican woman with an arthritic hip and a cast in one eye came into the room, keeping her gaze on the floor.

'Carmen, tell this stranger that Miss Bonnie ain't here. Tell him!'

The housekeeper fought for composure, and answered in a voice which was scarcely audible. '*Senorita* Bonnie, she is not here.'

Manton dismissed her and she left the room again, relief partially straightening her bent back. Sandy murmured thanks which he did not feel and acknowledged a suggestion that he could call at the cook house for coffee if he was thirsty.

He unhitched the skewbald without haste and looked about him. Most of the hands were away on the range, tending the cattle. The state of the buildings showed that the spread was being efficiently run. But there was some sort of tension about the outfit. Something hard to pin down.

As he rode away towards town, Sandy found himself reflecting that Bonnie was better away from it.

During the first half-mile coming away, the young man's spirits were low, but after that he gradually brighened. His investigator's bump of curiosity began to take over from his temporary melancholy. Clearly, all was not well with the Box M, even if it was making a useful profit.

Where did that tension spring from? If the Mantons had troubles, were they anything remotely to do with the Hickstead killing and Sandy's profes- sional business?

He was disappointed in not having contacted Bonnie again, and he wondered if he was a long way from her at Conchas Creek. Would she have told the two killers where her home was on so brief an acquaintance as theirs must have been?

Was he wasting Hickstead's money?

One item which really hurt his pride was being caught by the cow hand while he was spying on the buildings through his glass. He wanted to do something to boost his morale in the light of that setback. He promised himself that if the opportunity presented itself, he would do a little more snooping on Box M property and the next time he would not be caught.

7

The bubbling laughter started in the kitchen when Sandy Crease's receding figure was about one hundred yards away. Jeff Manton started away from the window where he had been watching the withdrawal. For a few seconds his tanned face blanched, but gradually he recovered his poise and moved towards the door which led to the back of the house.

By that time, Bonnie's voice was trilling through all its cadences. It had a singular effect upon all who heard it: even her close kin like Jeff. He stepped into the kitchen, glared fiercely at the Mexican woman who had just asserted that Bonnie was nowhere about, and then blinked in the direction of his sister.

'How about that then, big brother? Did I give you a surprise, or did I give you a surprise?'

Bonnie was dodging back and forth on the rear side of a stove pipe. Her face was flushed through healthy outdoor exercise, but she still looked full of energy and nothing that had happened recently seemed to bother her at all. Jeff could not help envying her ability to put troublesome matters of great moment to the back of her mind.

He studied her. Obviously, she had been riding. She had on a black shirt and matador pants. Her hair on this occasion was topped by a squarely-placed grey stetson with a flat crown. She laughed some more, her green eyes mocking him all the while.

In spite of himself Jeff was forced to grin back at her. He moved forward across the working area and attempted to catch hold of her. She dodged him around the stove pipe, but allowed herself to be caught at the second attempt.

They shared a fleeting embrace before Jeff led the way into the front room and gestured for her to sit down. This time he glared at her and she dropped into an armchair to placate him.

'Things have been happenin', sis.'

'I'd be the first to agree to that,' Bonnie murmured.

She pulled off her hat, and tossed her hair up. She was minus the holding ribbon and combing it vigorously when Jeff broke in upon her thoughts again.

'Why in tarnation did you have to come into this house in secret? Did you do it to avoid that fellow who's jest left? Are you in some sort of trouble?'

Bonnie paused in her grooming. She pouted her lips and peered at him through eyelashes almost too long to be real.

'I came secretly, brother, jest because you're always pridin' yourself that no one can get near this house without you knowin' first. And what's more, I could get as far as the buildings unobserved again, if I felt like it. As for that other business, I came here because I wanted to. I had no idea that anyone else was headed for this ranch, an' I certainly didn't tell anyone to follow me.'

Jeff took a little time to absorb what she had said, but he still had questions to ask.

'He said his name was Crease. Sandy Crease. Does he mean anything to you?'

'He's jest a young man who lives in a town where I put some money into a shop, that's all. I was on speakin' terms with him. I danced with him in the barn. And that was all.'

After lighting a stogie, Jeff asked casually, 'What do you know about a murder in Drovers' Halt?'

Bonnie blinked. 'Oh, some fellow at the hotel was stabbed with a fancy dagger. Name of Hickstead. A visitor from Colorado, I think. He was buried in the town. More than that I can't say. You don't take me for a murderer on the run, do you?'

Ignoring the last question, the brother went on: 'Do you have any reason to suppose that the murderers might have come the same way as you did?'

His tone had turned brusque. Bonnie knew better than to give him a flippant reply. 'No, why on earth should they? I've probably spoken to them like a lot of other men, in the town, maybe at the dance, but that's all.'

Jeff was about to follow up this statement with a further question but he held off long enough for the Mexican servant to put a tray of coffee gear on the table and withdraw.

'Crease said they gave you two rubies. Is that so?'

'How would I know?' the girl responded offhandedly.

'Darn it, Bonnie, this is important! Don't answer me like that! After all, you and me, we've had enough trouble in the past year or two!'

'I wouldn't know because I didn't see who put the two stones under the door of my shop! That's why I answered you in that fashion. So can we stop the cross-examination now because I'm tired?'

Suddenly, Jeff was tired himself. He shrugged and rose to his feet again. 'Are you plannin' on stayin' any length of time?' His tone had changed.

Bonnie rose and stretched and flexed her arms. 'Shucks, I could do with a bath.' She yawned rather prettily, arching her long neck. 'You want to know if I'm staying? I don' know myself yet, brother. Ask me again a bit later. Right now I want a bath more than anything else.'

The door at the rear had opened, the servant having heard what she had said. At the same time, Bonnie had a bright idea. 'I don't think I'll bathe in the house. I'll go along to the bathin' creek an' gradually cool down there.'

Jeff started to say: 'You'll be safer cleanin' up here — '

Bonnie turned on him, however, with a sudden flash of temper. 'I'll bathe where I said I'll bathe, an' I won't have anybody along with me as an escort, either. I've told you once not to expect anyone about the range who shouldn't be here. Now, stop pesterin' me. You hear?'

'All right, sis, if that's the way you want it. We'll be lookin' out for you around time for the evenin' meal. Or will it limit you too much if you have to say yes to that?'

The girl's anger subsided as quickly as it had appeared. She apologised, blushed rather becomingly and glanced at herself in the mirror on the wall over the fireplace. Some of the colour in her face was there because she had lied, but she did not think that Jeff would know that.

Her eyes glanced sideways at the big portrait of her father, the founder of the ranch. He gave her his probing steady stare, as always. The Mantons had been good and strong as long as he was alive. He looked like Abe Lincoln in his heyday. But after old Rick Manton had died, things had unbelievingly turned bad for the surviving Mantons.

Jeff said: 'I've got work to do.'

He was about to step through the

kitchen when Bonnie arrested his progress by suddenly clearing her throat rather obviously. He came back into the room and wondered what she wanted.

'Is 'you-know-who' expected, Jeff?'

The rancher's sober features underwent a change. His expression hardened, ageing him some five years. 'Harte Jonas doesn't come around all that often, but he still has his talons into us. I'd give anything to get him off our backs, an' that's for sure. If you go into town at all, keep away from him.'

This tone of voice suggested that the girl was being given an order. Curiously enough, she did not object to it. This time, Jeff merely nodded and then he went on his way. Shortly after he had gone, the servant came in almost silently, carrying a tray of fresh fruit pie. Bonnie acknowledged her and took a big slice, although for some reason she did not feel hungry.

The girl, left on her own, subsided in the chair which had been the favourite of her father. Swinging one leg, she munched the food and studied the portrait on the wall. Her thoughts, however, were on other people.

Five years had elapsed since Rick Manton died. It seemed like an age. For a time, Martha, Rick's wife, managed to hold things together. After about a year, instead of getting over his passing she seemed to mourn all the more, withdrawing into herself and becoming absent-minded.

During a spell away from the ranch she had met a well-to-do travelling gentleman by the name of Harte Jonas, and this meeting had really been the undoing of the children of the marriage. Martha had warned him when he started to pay court to her that she was not really interested in any other man. That sort of talk had not put him off, and when he persisted a little of his charm worked on her and she began to wonder if in fact there was room for another man on the Box M which Rick had fashioned out of his own energies and ability.

Jeff and Bonnie had not wanted to put anything in their mother's way, and she was careful — so she thought — of their interests. After a fairly long courtship, she agreed to marriage, but made it clear at the outset that the Box M stayed the Box M, and that her second husband, Jonas, did not assume control.

In a rather subtle way, he had got round her. He advised her to write her wishes into a new will, at the same time making provision for him, Jonas, in the event that she did not outlive him. And so it was put into writing if Martha died first, her children were to retain control and possession of the ranch, and that Harte, her second husband, was to receive from the estate ten thousand dollars a year during his lifetime.

At first, Jeff and Bonnie had thought that he might tire of their mother because she was in no way so attractive as she had been in their father's day, but Harte Jonas had patience. He stayed around and, after two years, his patience was rewarded.

Martha contracted a critical illness and died within a week or two. It was then that trouble started for the younger generation. Jonas was entitled to ten thousand dollars a year out of the profits from the ranch and he insisted upon being paid every penny, rather than ploughing some of his funds back into the venture as some men might have done.

In the months immediately after the burial of Martha, Jonas did no work around the ranch. He merely moved around, allowing the hired hands to get a good look at him and was critical of Jeff's efforts. The time came when Bonnie grew very restless. She took off one day, and because she was not absolutely necessary to the running of the spread Jonas made no attempt to have her brought back.

In time, Jonas's own restlessness and need for a change made him take himself off to the nearest town and stay there more or less permanently. His departure afforded Jeff some relief, but the stepfather stayed in the area, preying upon the spread like a human vulture and quite soon the annual withdrawal of funds for Jonas's private pocket began to have an adverse effect upon the ranch as a going concern.

Jeff had to cut down upon his expenditure. Wages suffered and so the atmosphere gradually changed. Bonnie used her talents as she travelled. Her father's sterling character kept her going and only her restlessness prevented her from settling somewhere permanently and making something worthwhile of herself.

The food long since finished, Bonnie began to kick the fireside with the blunt toe of her half-boot. Presently, a stogie rolled off the mantelpiece and fell in the hearth. She retrieved it, examined it and finally put a match to it while her thoughts ranged backwards and forwards over Jeff's problems and her own.

She drew easily on the smoke, tackling the cigar like a man.

From Harte Jonas, the hated one, her thoughts slipped back to her experiences in Drovers' Halt. There, at times, she had enjoyed herself. Moreover, her business had prospered. But it had been the two elusive young men, Clancy Dune and Roger Brand, who had really appealed to her and recharged her restlessness. She knew that if they had committed murder she ought to feel repelled by the thought of them: and yet she did not. She had a woman's sneaking admiration for men who knew what they wanted and took steps to get it. Harte Jonas was the one man she had known who did not share this admiration she had for villains.

Jonas remained an enemy, forever.

She had lied to Jeff about the possibility of the two hunted men turning up in the vicinity of the Box M. Captivated by their conversational powers, the pull of the sad lilting songs sung to the guitar, she had taken some pains to make sure that they knew exactly how to get to Conchas Creek and the Box M ranch which lay beyond the town.

She wondered what it would be like to have such a couple as allies. She smiled to herself as she imagined their taking a hand in the affair of the Mantons versus Harte Jonas.

Was it possible, she wondered, to talk them into helping her to rid the Mantons of their unwanted enemy?

At that point, her restlessness returned. She recollected that she wanted to bathe. If she didn't start soon, the urge would have left her. Feeling quite sure of herself again, she collected towels from the servant and wandered out of doors to the grey mare which awaited her, ill at ease due to its earlier labours.

8

A Box M isolated line cabin lay to the south-east of the spread at a point usually regarded as being too distant from the buildings for anyone to keep a special lookout near it. Shortly after dawn that morning, the most sought-after men in Raton County had moved into it using the utmost caution.

Now, late in the afternoon they were rested, reasonably well fed but still a little unsure of themselves on this territory which was hostile to strangers and to which they were unused. Around four o'clock, Roger Brand, the younger of the two young renegades, stopped plucking the strings of his guitar and laid it aside.

He was reclining on an old cow-hide stretched across the floor. His partner, Clancy Dune, was reclining on the upper of two bunks not far from a window which revealed quite a good part of the nearby range. Clancy never looked anything but cool, this time was no exception.

'So what gives, pardner?' he asked sleepily.

'After all, I don't think it was wise to follow the girl's instructions for gettin' into this part of the world!'

Dune did not share his passion for the argument. He blinked his blue eyes at a spider which was spinning a web around the angle of a ceiling beam and idly wondered how long the small creature would be busy before the job was done.

'In your excitement, you had to throw that Spanish dagger,' he murmured. 'Remember? Every time you do that sort of thing we have to up and away. An' sometimes, it ain't all that convenient. I wanted to stay there an' get to know that Bonnie a whole lot better.

'Now, you're havin' doubts about comin' here. You'll allow Drovers' Halt would not have been exactly healthy for us if we'd stayed there till dawn, after what you did in that hotel room?'

'Quit ridin' me, Clan,' Brand protested, 'you knew what sort of a man I was when you agreed to become my pardner. It ain't that. I mean this place might not be healthy. Folks in town talked about givin' it a wide berth these days. Something's wrong around here, an' we don't know what it is.'

Dune shifted his legs rather suddenly. One of his boots connected with a whisky bottle, already half empty. He took a swig from the neck of the bottle, glanced rather pointedly at his partner and then tossed the bottle to him.

Brand took a big mouthful and gargled with it before swallowing.

Dune remarked: 'When we left Drovers' Halt it was a matter of comin' away rather than goin' anywhere special. We had to be out of it, an' we made it away when the borders were sealed with peace officers dyin' to meet up with us. So I don't see how you can grumble if we're still not apprehended an' hidden on Box M territory.

'I had a distinct feelin' that the girl intended to come this way real soon, an' I may yet be proved right. There was something about our style appealed to her. Fair enough, what happened to Hickstead might have cooled her interest forever, but every now and again there's a female who's ardour still remains, even after a killin'.

'Those are the kind for us. If she does show up, she'll be with us one hundred per cent, as the moneyed hombres say.'

Brand gave himself a smoke. He was thoughtful for a while, and before he spoke again he studied the profile of his partner as though seeing him closely for the first time. 'Jest supposin' like you say she comes this way, an' Hickstead's death ain't soured her. Who do you suppose she'll take to? You or me? After all, we're pardners, an' two men and one woman is a difficult sort of combination if we ever intend doin' any travellin' or anything with her. How would it be, do you think?'

'Roger, there's no man on earth can ever answer in detail questions about a woman he doesn't know terribly well. We'll jest have to wait and see, won't we? There's a chance it might not turn out to be an ordinary man and woman relationship, after all.'

'What other sort of relationship is there?'

Brand felt a trifle naïve as he asked his question, and Dune was slow to answer it. At length, he remarked: 'Oh, I wasn't thinkin' of anything unusual. Jest that it might be a business relationship, that's all. Business, Rog. After all, that girl had a mighty fine little store workin' for her in Drovers' Halt, an' she can use a knife to fashion things with, too. The main difference between her an' you is that she works mostly on wood while you use flesh.'

Brand was in no hurry to answer. Instead, he juggled the corked bottle between his feet.

'We have this constant problem,' Dune remarked, after a time. 'Funds. We need a fair amount of foldin' money. The obvious thing is to cash in on the stones Hickstead so kindly bequeathed to us, but it ain't likely we're goin' to get a lot for them.'

'Tryin' to sell them might be dangerous,' Brand put in quickly. 'They might lead the sheriff's men back to us. But I agree with you that we may not get much for them. Seems I heard tell they have to be cut by an expert to make them valuable. Cuttin' an' matchin', so I've heard.'

'Maybe the girl could help in disposin' of them,' Dune murmured.

Brand was getting riled because most of what his partner was saying was based on supposition. He opened his mouth to say as much, but something about the tense way in which Dune was staring out of the window made him hold back.

'How would you like to gamble five

dollars Bonnie Manton ain't anywhere near here?' Dune suggested lightly.

Brand got up and looked out of the window. There was Bonnie, mounted on the back of a grey mare which looked as if it had been pushed hard earlier in the day.

'So she's here, after all,' the guitar player conceded.

He moved back a foot or two so as to be less conspicuous and started to run his long sensitive fingers over the short, down-drooping moustache and chin beard, as though he was checking his outward appearance by the sense of touch.

'Think she knows we're here?' Brand wanted to know.

'I doubt it,' Dune reasoned. 'She has a big towel draped round her shoulders. I'd say she came this way specially to bathe somewhere. In any case, we'll soon know. She's plannin' to use the cabin for a changin' room.'

The partners had hidden their horses rather cleverly, although they were not far from the cabin. Consequently, as there was no fire in the building Bonnie had no idea that she was about to have company until she smelled the whisky and was grabbed by the agile pair waiting for her.

Brand got to her first. If she had gone off them due to the murder, he would have been the first one to know it. Bonnie tensed, not at first knowing who they were, but as soon as she realised that the arms gripping her belonged to the young guitarist, she relaxed again and waltzed around the cleared part of the floor, kissing Brand and being kissed by him.

Clancy Dune hummed a tune which they all knew, awaited his opportunity to cut in and at once took over from Brand, who was almost breathless with excitement. Dune stayed in command for a while and it was the strumming of the guitar strings which made the whirling couple give up and seat themselves on the bottom bunk.

'Oh, shucks, boys. I'm delighted you

felt you could come! But you sure did take me by surprise. At first I thought you might be a young man from Drovers' Halt who's been up to the house looking for me. Ain't I glad it's you, though, an' not him!'

Bonnie's revelation had the effect of making the men tense up.

'Did he come lookin' for you personally, Bonnie?' Dune queried. 'I mean as a man might follow a woman?'

Bonnie glanced briefly at each of them. 'It's difficult to know how to answer your question. I know he's interested in me because he's been more than passin' attentive before I left his hometown, but jest what his motives are in comin' all this way, I don't know.'

'They'll have a reward out for us by this time,' Brand observed in a neutral voice.

'That's so, boys, but this young fellow, Sandy Crease ain't likely to give you much trouble. He ain't the sort to make a success of things. It's his brother who's the town marshal. The folks don't think an awful lot of Sandy, although he did ride out of town a piece an' almost got himself shot to pieces. I suppose it was you he encountered near some hogsback ridge?'

Dune and Brand exchanged glances. They did not need to nod to answer Bonnie's question. Neither of them thought that Sandy was a pushover, as his hometown appeared to do. The killers were surprised to know that he had survived his fall from the ridge side. If he could come up after that, he had to have some sand in his craw.

In spite of Bonnie's obvious attraction for him, Dune returned to his observation spot on the top bunk. 'We've been talkin' about riskin' selling certain stones, an' what we might be able to raise on them,' he explained conversationally.

The girl remained seated on the lower bunk with her legs stretched out provocatively in the matador pants. 'You have problems, boys, an' I know what they are. You want to keep out of the clutches of the law, get your hands on some ready funds, and so on.

'Maybe the three of us could help each other. If you feel you could trust me. We Mantons have trouble, as well. There's this hombre, Harte Jonas, my stepfather, bleedin' the ranch of ten thousand dollars a year, an' believe me, the profits won't stand it. Another year like the two we've jest had an' the spread will be on the rocks.

'Harte Jonas hangs around in town, lookin' for easy money. He's jest the sort of hombre who might pay a good price for your bag of stones. Now, what do you say to tryin' to sell them to him?'

Clearly, both men were keen to trust the girl, but each of them could see snags in her suggestion. They hesitated to argue and Bonnie had to use the persuasion of her finely arched brows to draw comment out of them.

Brand cracked his knuckles. 'If we went into town, we could be spotted by someone anxious for reward money.'

'An' why should your stepfather pay a lot of money for our uncut stones, particularly as he wouldn't know where they come from?'

Dune sounded the more assured of the two, and it was clear by his expression that he was prepared to hear more from Bonnie.

'I believe I could so work it that you wouldn't be recognised, and Harte Jonas would buy the stones because he thought they were the key to untold riches.'

Dune whistled. 'You're a sorceress, Bonnie, an' no mistake, if you can fix things like that. But what would you get out of the deal? You haven't mentioned yourself yet.'

Bonnie indulged in a little of her own particular brand of laughter. 'I'd have helped a couple of good friends, and also I would have achieved some satisfaction. Besides, if Jonas ever really got to thinkin' he was on the verge of discoverin' a whole lot of money, we could do almost anything with him. Anything!'

'Like getting rid of him altogether?' Brand surmised mildly.

'Even that,' the girl murmured.

She was just starting to laugh again when Dune began to show signs of restlessness on the top bunk, where he was still acting as look-out. Clearly, he had seen something else and this time he had two people gripped by curiosity. Bonnie and Brand came up behind him as he raised an arm to hold them back.

'Is it my mare, or something? What's worryin' you, Clan? Are we observed?'

Bonnie showed more excitement than actual anxiety. At first, neither she nor Brand could see what it was that Dune had observed. Brand was told to get the spyglass, which he did very promptly, poking it into Dune's hand because the latter did not want to shift the line of his gaze.

'Bright reflected sunlight, Bonnie. That's all so far. But it could mean an awful lot. I have to ask you this. You came along here with that towel around your shoulders. Did any of the boys from the ranch know what you were plannin' to do?'

Bonnie moved the pointed tip of her tongue around her full lips as she toyed with the question. She shrugged rather prettily.

'It's possible, I suppose. Usually, the ordinary hands wouldn't risk watchin' me bathe, but I haven't been at home for a long time. You think somebody might have followed me up from the building to take a look?'

Brand studied her face and was surprised to detect that she was not particularly embarrassed at the idea of a Peeping Tom. Dune nodded. After that, the silence built up in the cabin for nearly two minutes. Finally, the observer grunted in a positive sort of way and turned the glass over to his partner.

'Over there, in those trees. The fellow is very nicely camouflaged but he's also watchin'. What I must have seen earlier was the reflection of the sun on his spyglass lens. We can safely assume that he's on his own, but even so he's a menace to us. We can't be sure it's you he's after seein'. He might have been onto us from earlier today. So what do we do about him? We can't come out until he's moved on, so we *have* to do something. What do you suggest, Bonnie? You're the local.'

'I don't think for a minute he could have been aware of your presence,' the girl reasoned. 'Don't forget I was very wide awake an' I didn't detect anything. Assume he's lookin' for me. I'll show him where I am in a short while.'

Bonnie already had a shrewd idea who it was amid the trees observing the shack. There was a fairly well known landmark around the east side of Manton range in the form of a dried-out *arroyo*. The stream bed had been there for years and it stretched for a mile or more from north-east to around to south-east, where the line cabin was located.

Probably the rider had ridden along the *arroyo* from the northern end;

which would account for his sudden appearance in that particular clump of trees.

'Was there something else you wanted to do first?' Brand asked curiously. His fingers were working on his facial hair again.

'About our plan. I want you to disguise yourselves as ordinary prospectors before you go to town. Then you have to look out for Harte Jonas. Remember the name. It's important. If you find me a piece of paper and a pencil I'll draw you a little map. You must tell him that you want to raise money on the stones you have with you, an' also you need a few thousand to buy stores to take you back to the scene of your 'field' in the Bad Lands.'

Brand produced the paper and pencil from inside his hat and handed them to her. He was mildly put out when his partner handed to him the spyglass and insisted on his keeping watch while the writing was done. Brand performed his task with a bad grace. Meanwhile,

Bonnie flattened the paper on the table top and clearly started to think out what she was going to draw.

Presently, she started work with the pencil. She drew three shapes to represent the mouths of canyons and slowly wrote across all three, in block capitals, *Triple Canyon*. She was absorbed in her work and flattered that Dune should show such an interest.

'Is there really a place called Triple Canyon?' he asked.

Bonnie nodded. 'And for the purpose of this bit of business your diamond field is located somewhere beyond the mouths.' She went on drawing. 'I want you to refuse to give Jonas the actual location of the field when you first do business. That'll make him all the more keen. Most likely he'll jest have to follow you to the field an' then, maybe, we can lose him.'

'Is that all we need to know now?' Dune asked.

'I think so, Clan. Take this paper with you. If you think he needs coaxin' to follow you, drop this map where he can find it. Or something. Me, I'm going to make sure that this observer doesn't see you. You must move off this territory while I have his attention. Okay?'

'I guess so, as you're callin' the tune at this time, Bonnie,' Dune approved. 'But how do you fit in with this canyon business?'

'I'll join you later. Jonas mustn't catch sight of me while you're doin' business with him, otherwise he might guess there's something wrong. Now, is there anything else before I get started?'

It was obvious to Bonnie that her new business partners would have thought nothing of eliminating the watcher in the trees and coming along themselves with her to the bathing spot. However, their life on the run had taught them when to be cautious and this time, evidently, was one for discretion.

Murmuring their approval, they withdrew well away from window and door and watched her move out into the open.

9

Before Bonnie came out from the line cabin and trotted across to where the grey mare was cropping grass, Sandy Crease had backed his tired mount further into the trees and given it a rough rub down with torn-up grass. He was smiling to himself now, having recognised the elusive girl's regular riding horse.

As he started to come away from the Box M buildings, he had looked around for some sort of route diversion. Presently, the area in regular use for cattle range had dropped behind and when he was fairly sure that he was no longer observed, he turned away from his north-easterly route and some time later stumbled upon the dried-out stream bed.

A terrific desire to discover something about the sprawl of ranch land had made him follow it all its length, and in so doing he had put himself within a short distance of the line cabin and the three people he was principally interested in.

He had no means of knowing that Bonnie had been at the ranch house after he left, or that she had company in the isolated building. But he knew that he had renewed contact and that bit of progress had made him feel good.

He could now telegraph his home-town and inform the man who was employing him that progress was being made.

With the grass he worked hard on the skewbald's body, doing what he could to refresh it from the rigours of the day. He was crouched and working on the legs when the door of the cabin opened rather noisily and the young female he was anxious to see emerged.

Sandy straightened up, feeling rather out of breath. He had intended to make proper contact in the shack, but now Bonnie was moving with haste and he wondered if she was up to anything worth watching before he showed himself. He shrugged, not being sure what to do. At the same time he was watchful. For a woman who could have no idea that she was observed, she certainly moved in an attractive sort of way.

Standing beside the mare some fifty yards away with her feet slightly apart, she raised the coloured bath towel which had been draped around her shoulders and gently flapped it to fan herself. Draped as she was in the black shirt and matador pants she looked more like a bull-fighter than ever before.

Humming a melody from old Spain, she inserted her left boot toe into the stirrup and agilely swung herself up. Sandy filled his lungs and prepared to shout, but something made him desist at the last moment. Instead, he rested his bulk on the back of the skewbald and thought about making a short ride to see what she was about.

There was no doubt in his mind that she was planning to bathe. That sort of observation was probably one of a detective's most interesting perks. While one part of his mind enthused about the prospect, another part counselled caution. After all, he had stumbled upon her quite unawares, and there might just possibly be someone else on Box M land acting as an escort to the girl.

He finished making the horse ready for a move as quickly as possible and while the mare up ahead was still well within earshot, he started the pursuit. As he rode, he found his thoughts going back and forward over his assignment. If he had made this long journey and only managed to contact the girl his report to Hickstead would seem ludicrous, and yet he found himself hoping that the killers had no longer any active part in her life.

The bathing pool was a spot where a narrow minor stream had broadened out and grown deeper. A one-time buffalo wallow had become filled with the steady-flowing creek water and so provided a remote but pleasant place for human bathing.

A thin ring of stunted oak trees marked the place where the pool lay, and much lower, fringing the water's edge, weeping willows afforded another screen and a place in which to change.

The gentle sounds of the water carried to Sandy's ears and made him go slower. The mare and girl had long since disappeared into the screen of oaks when he dismounted and took the skewbald by the head. It seemed churlish to tether the horse with a pin so near to the water and yet so far away, but he was not yet sure of the situation down at the water's edge.

He hesitated about taking his Winchester along with him, and finally left it in the scabbard, strolling down the gentle slope with only his .45 to defend himself with. Minus his spurs he made very little sound. His nerves played small tricks as he neared the inner ring of willows, but nothing happened to make him draw the gun or to make him think that the girl had any other human there with her.

The first thing he noticed was the pair of matador pants hanging mysteriously from a group of swaying pendent twigs. Keen-eyed he watched everything. The swish of the mare's tail in the shallows across the pool took him by surprise and almost made him think there *were* other humans present.

Hidden by the many drooping fronds, Bonnie started to hum to herself. She tested the shallow waters down the bank and this brought from her a few subdued trills of laughter. Sandy felt guilty of keeping his presence a secret in the circumstances, standing as he was no more than twenty feet away. He cleared his throat rather noisily and softly called the girl by name but, she appeared not to notice. It was almost as if fate had decreed that he should get the most out of the peep show.

The flat-topped grey stetson came skimming out of cover straight towards him, but before he could catch his breath a half-seen body straightened out on the water's edge and entered the foaming surface in a neat dive.

Bonnie made no more noise than a leaping salmon, and then she was gone in a long dive beneath the surface, trailing bubbles as her lithe body headed swiftly towards the other side of the pool. Sandy had his mouth puckered for a whistle when he stepped through the screen of drooping fronds and watched the pool from the spot where the girl had undressed.

The pull of her attraction was working on him then, and almost unconsciously he was aware of his own inner yearning to freshen up in the bubbling creek. Hatless, he stared down into the depths. Most of the water looked a dark green in the shadowed sunlight of late afternoon, but Bonnie's surfacing body changed that. First, she was a pale green herself. As she came nearer the surface her colour lost its green tinge and returned to the healthy pink of every day.

Suddenly the head broke surface. The long bell of hair, thoroughly soaked, was swept back by the waters so that it fitted tightly against her skull and draped itself down the back of her long shapely neck.

Sandy called to her while her head was still facing the other way. She smoothed back her hair and appeared not to have heard. There was greater urgency in his voice as he called a second time.

'Bonnie! It's me, Sandy! I thought you ought to know you've got company!'

This time, she stiffened and turned in the water, kicking out easily with her legs while she stared at him apparently in open wonder. Womanlike, her hand went to her breast. She coughed on a mouthful of swallowed water, arched her brows and shifted her position in the pool until she was facing him in the breast-stroke position with her body immersed to chin level.

'Well, I do declare. Sandy Crease in the flesh. Many miles from home an' watchin' a lady at her bathin'. Sandy I sure do hope you didn't follow me all the way from Drovers' Halt jest to see me take a bath? That sure would be something, wouldn't it?

'I still can't rightly figure how you've popped up like that right in the middle of Box M property, but no doubt you can explain! If you are hot as you look, you'd better strip off an' get in this water yourself!'

Sandy waved his arms about in a neutral sort of gesture. There was a wicked glint in the green eyes as he hesitated. Bonnie flared her nostrils and sought words with which to embarrass him.

'Oh, well, suit yourself. If you only came to watch I hope you enjoy yourself!'

Shrugging easily in the bubbling water, she did one strong arm stroke with each arm and then dipped the upper part of her body in a surface dive. She disappeared from view, legs last in a gesture laid on specially for him. Hair fanned out like dark weed as she went lower and still lower, and approached the bank on which he stood. Her shape tantalisingly became diffused as he watched, but he had seen enough and heard enough to know that now was a time to put the job and other considerations aside.

Dune and Brand were almost forgotten as Sandy stripped down to his newly-acquired riding denims and plunged in himself. Wriggling like a fish, Bonnie easily avoided him, moving among the tree roots on the near side.

Sandy came up gasping and finger-combing his hair which had considerably lengthened during his travels. As soon as he had his breath back he grinned and swam under the pendent branches of the willow, splashing Bonnie as she reappeared.

'Sure is a fine spot to bathe, Bonnie!

I wonder why you ever left the home spread in the first place?'

He was asking a question and yet not expecting an answer while they were still in the water. Bonnie made a lunge at him and managed to push his head under. Before he could recover she had crossed the deep pool and shown him the strength of her arm and leg movements.

He found that he could match her for speed, but only with an effort and presently his early efforts in the saddle made him tire of chasing her. He was ready to take a rest. Up on the high ground, the skewbald whinnied plaintively. Bonnie, who wanted an excuse to send him away while she left the water at once remonstrated with him.

'Doggone it, Sandy, have you tethered that poor horse within the sight of fresh water? Shame on you if you don't go up there an' loosen him straight away!'

In his waterlogged state, Sandy was not keen to go, but the bleak look was

140

there in Bonnie's remarkable green eyes and he thought it best to fall in with her wishes. As soon as he was up the slope, trailing water from his denims, she slipped from the pool and started to towel herself down.

Sandy removed the saddle before turning the skewbald loose and by the time he was back down the slope in the wake of the excited horse the girl had wriggled into her matador pants and was buttoning on her shirt.

The young man swam for two minutes more. He then left the skewbald to drink and take its exercise and came out to get dressed again. He used his spare shirt as a towel and as soon as he was partially dry he came out from the willows, intent upon talking.

'I suppose you an' me meetin' here is what folks call a mighty big coincidence,' he observed, with a broad grin.

Bonnie was kneeling on the slope, outlining her eyes and nose with the edge of the towel. 'I'll go along with that statement, amigo, seein' as how you're so far away from home an' you ain't supposed to know anything about Box M territory.'

A short interesting silence grew up between them while each tried to figure out exactly how much the other was personally attracted.

'I've already been to the ranch askin' for you,' Sandy admitted rather lamely. 'I had a talk with your brother, but he didn't have a whole lot to say.'

The girl sat down and busied herself with a long comb and her thoughts. She knew that Sandy was quite shrewd in some ways and also that he was not lacking in courage. If he guessed anywhere near the truth he would assuredly put his life in danger again and although she was not strongly attracted to him she did not want him to come to a sudden end on Manton property.

'What sort of an excuse did you give my brother for comin' here? You were followin' me, weren't you, Sandy?'

Feeling his colour mounting, the young man averted his face. 'I told him you might be associatin' with killers, men who have stolen quite a quantity of semi-precious stones.'

'An' was Jeff impressed?' she asked calmly.

'I have to admit that he wasn't. He treated me like an intruder an' acted all the time as if the outfit was under some sort of threat. If there was anything here that a friend could help with, you'd be sure to mention it, wouldn't you, Bonnie?'

She nodded without conviction. 'You have a lively imagination, Sandy. You can sense an atmosphere when there isn't one, an' you seem to have made up your mind I'd associate with undesirables on the slightest pretext. Now that I'm assurin' you that all's well, what will you do? Will you head right back home again?'

Sandy's expression hardened. 'No, I'm not goin' straight home. I'm workin' for Senator Hickstead at the

143

moment, an' he expects me to keep on lookin' for the men who killed his brother. I shall certainly stay out in the open until I make some sort of progress in my search. The old man wouldn't expect me to give up so quickly.'

Bonnie stretched out on her back and put her hands behind her head. She stayed in that provocative position for a while, wondering just how far Sandy trusted her. He was fully aware of her, but judging by the changing expression on his face her feminine wiles were not quite a match for his sense of duty.

Feeling slightly annoyed, the girl stopped trying to ensnare him. Instead, she fished out of her hat band two of brother Jeff's stogies and offered one to her restless companion. This time he did relax and they remained for another ten minutes, seated side by side under the willow fronds, calmly enjoying the taste of cigars.

The girl thought about the cabin, until so recently the hiding place of Sandy's worst enemies. She smiled about the situation and a sudden inner perverseness made her want to go back there and take her companion with her.

Presently, she stood up. 'I'm going back to the cabin now,' she explained.

Without comment, Sandy began to pack up. He overtook her on the ride and followed her close as they came out of the timber stand to approach the shack. Unbeknown to him, Bonnie was having a last minute attack of nerves in case her other contacts had not departed as quickly as she had anticipated.

She dismounted first and slipped indoors, her bright eyes looking for obvious signs of the previous occupants and their belongings. They had gone and they had left nothing except for the empty whisky bottle. She breathed easily again, squatting on the lower bunk and wondering what Sandy would make of the place.

The young man only came as far as the doorway. He had his hand on his revolver in the holster and his expression had materially changed. The lazy look had left his blue eyes. He looked years older than when he had visited her in Drovers' Halt.

'There's a lot of fresh horse tracks outside here, Bonnie. Two men at least left here jest a short time ago. I think you've made a fool of me. Maybe you're fooling your brother, too.'

'What do you mean, exactly?' she asked quietly.

'I mean you led me away from this place when it was occupied. On purpose. I think it's possible the killers I was sent after have been here an' that you know a whole lot more about their business than you've told anybody. You're ridin' for a fall, young lady, an' no mistake!'

If he had taken two steps into the building he felt that he would have laid hands on her and given her a good shaking, at the least. But he backed out, leaving the door ajar, and while he was mounting up, his youthful face a repulsive scowl, she followed him to the door and started to laugh.

Once again strong emotion had triggered off her enigmatic laughter, and obscured her true feelings. Sandy felt that he was being mocked by it and he made haste to get away before his temper went out of control. The laughter followed him, making him spur the skewbald to greater effort.

When he was out of earshot, Bonnie suddenly went quiet. She had wanted to call after him that she had done him a favour, but it was too late.

10

After clearing the cabin and the area of the *arroyo* Sandy made a big detour, aiming to work his way around to the north side of the range again, on his way back to Conchas Creek. For a time he was really hard on the skewbald, making it work the harder because he had been so recently deceived.

Perhaps a half-hour later, he began to see that he was not doing the animal or himself any real good. He had been duped, but the girl who had duped him was clever and she had not succeeded altogether in her purpose, so a little had been gained during that protracted day.

Besides, while he was burning up energy on the return ride he might just be leaving himself open to his enemies, who could be travelling in the same direction. For a time, his reason had suffered. Instead of being so angry with the girl he ought to have attempted to find out where the riders had gone.

One consideration, however, could be discarded. Jeff Manton was no friend of the killers. Sandy felt sure of that. The young boss of the Box M would not shelter them even to accommodate his only sister. So they must have cleared Box M range, or moved themselves to some spot equally remote in another part of it.

Still angry with himself, Sandy headed back for Conchas Creek. He had a hankering after a night in a real bed. After that, he would renew his search and send a message to his employer. He wondered how Drovers' Halt had settled down since his departure, but it was hard to visualise the place now. Anyway, it would be different with Jacob S. Hickstead breathing down the necks of the other male Creases.

When eventually the skewbald carried him up the dirt of Main Street, he felt more tired than he had done before the bathe in the pool and lukewarm beer had a great attraction for him even though the saloons were noisy. He drank one glass and reluctantly came away to book a hotel room and stable the horse before returning to imbibe considerably more liquor and make up for his lack of food during the day.

★   ★   ★

When they first left the line cabin Clancy Dune and Roger Brand rode towards the east. Had young Crease not been in such a hurry to get back to town, he might have ridden up their tracks and made contact that same evening. However, this was not to be.

Whatever else they were to each other, Dune and Brand were good companions. They could ride along in silence by the hour, or discuss current matters in detail without boring each other.

The meeting with Bonnie had given them a lot to think about. Uppermost in both their minds was the fact that she had not been put off them, even when she knew that they had killed at least once. Clearly, if they entertained the idea of bringing a young and attractive woman in to their short team they might encounter problems which had not bothered them so far.

Because she was of the opposite sex, she would obviously tend to favour one of them more than the other. That way led towards jealousy and when men were jealous they did not always make the right decisions or carry them out properly.

In the slow ride east, first one and then the other was on the point of putting into words a suggestion that Bonnie could spoil their partnership, and yet neither of them actually did say the things which would bring the matter out into the open.

'We'll not be droppin' her at this early stage, Roger, because she can be ruthless herself an' she admires ruthlessness in others. Us, for instance.

Whether we can wholly go along with the plan she outlined will remain to be seen. Right now, though, we'll see what we can do about changin' our appearance an' lookin' up this hombre she wants out of the way. You got any ideas how we might go about this operation?'

Brand slowed down his bay gelding and cocked one leg around the saddle horn. He picked away at a hollow tooth with a match stick. 'As we don't have any dressin' up clothes, that's the first consideration, I suppose. Either we acquire the clothes to dress up in out of town, or we get our hands on them when we get there.'

Dune was about to affirm that it would be better to enter town attired like prospectors when a new sound carried to their ears and radically changed their attitude to the immediate future. It was the raucous cry of a mule in torment. Or a mule being coaxed to do something it was not in favour of.

Brand readjusted his riding stance and spat out the match stick. 'Are you thinkin' what I'm thinkin', pardner?'

'We're well away from town now,' Dune observed, 'an' off Box M territory. An' some heaven-sent hombre has cut across our trail with a mule in tow. Seems to me I always heard prospectors couldn't operate without mules. Let's go take a look at the source of the noise.'

Dune's blue eyes were twinkling as he pressed his roan horse to a better speed and headed his partner towards a break in the trees which they were negotiating. Five minutes later, still hidden by the perimeter of the timber stand, they looked down into a narrow valley and saw an unusual sight. Two tall cottonwoods spanned the low-lying land to the northern end. Between them was a log cabin with green-painted shutters. To one side of the cabin and to some extent shadowed by smaller trees was a pole corral. Inside the corral were no less than three mules. The two which were calm and tethered to the posts were grey beasts, but the one which was threshing about with a couple of heavy panniers on its back had a pinkish shade to its hide and a devilish look in its eye.

The observers shared their interest between the animals and the old man who owned them and was in the process of training the third. The prospector looked to be in his sixties: of medium height with a long straggle of grey beard and a tall undented black stetson dusty enough to be nearly grey.

Dune started them forward. Side by side they rode slowly towards the corral taking in more detail. As they moved, the old man slowly gave ground, hanging on all the time to the head rope and muttering unprintable words which the mule might or might not have understood.

Eventually, the creature backed so far that its hind legs came up against the far side of the corral fence and that was when the old man made his move. He stepped closer, gave it a resounding kick in the side and looped the head rope to the nearest part of the fence, bringing it up short and appreciably out of breath.

The indignant creature stopped its noise and subsided against the fence, too tired even to demolish its panniers on the posts.

'Howdy, old timer!' Dune called in his heartiest voice.

The old man rose as if he had been stung from the bottom pole of the fence and turned to face his unbidden guests with a look of shocked surprise in his pale blue faded eyes. At once, he began to rub his horny hands down his bright red and green shirt, as though a clean handshake was a matter of prime importance.

'Welcome to Gunter's Empire, gents! Sorry I didn't see you before, but I was busy as you must have observed.'

Gunter came shuffling towards them on slightly bowed legs. He lifted his dusty hat in a nervous gesture and revealed that his crown was completely bald.

'I was thinkin' of makin' myself a bite

to eat, if you'd care to join me. What do you say, boys?'

Dune was the first to dismount. He introduced himself, using his christian name only and then gave that of his companion. Tex Gunter moved ahead of them to the door of the shack where they beheld a wooden plaque nailed to the frame.

It said:

This here is the property of one Tex Gunter, born in Texas and a visitor to almost everywhere else. Law-abiding guests are mostly welcome. Come on in.

Signed: *T.G.*

Chuckling to himself, the old man went indoors and began to put wood on the stove. He gave his guests time to knock the dust out of their clothes and indicated where they could wash if they so decided.

A half-hour later, the trio were seated at the well-scrubbed wooden table and eating hugely on bacon and tinned beans. Gunter's voice might have a piping quality to it at times, but nothing had impaired his appetite since his youth.

Dune slapped a few coins on the table before the meal was over and that gesture helped Tex to bring out his little secret treats. An hour later they were drinking whisky from a bottle with dust on the outside and building up to a good cloud of indoor smoke with a tobacco pipe and two cigars.

Tex was allowed to speak at some length about his travels in various states of the Union, but it was clear to him that his visitors had something on their minds which would have to be settled before the three of them turned in for the night.

At last, the old man yawned. He kicked the stove and the half-consumed wood inside it slowly collapsed to the bottom.

'Gents, I know you'll sleep well, but I have a feelin' there's something of a personal nature you want to talk about before we retire. I'm sorry if I've talked too long.'

He looked them over from his slumped position on a wall-side bench and their preoccupied expressions confirmed his impression. Here were two men who could be quite ruthless if they felt like it and they wanted to ask his help. At the time, Dune was cleaning his revolvers with an oily rag and Brand was carefully cutting his initials on a bare patch of the wall.

'It was good of you to broach the matter before turnin' in, Tex,' Dune remarked, moving his stogie further round his mouth. 'As a matter of fact, we have a bit of business to transact. We want to dress ourselves up in old clothes an' pass ourselves off as prospectors. It's only a short operation.'

Brand was smiling to give the old man confidence, but his expression changed on account of his partner's last remark. Obviously, at this stage Dune could not know how long or how short the operation was likely to be. There was a distinct likelihood that it would take a long time, if the two of them decided to carry out in detail Bonnie's plans to lure her stepfather out into the Bad Lands.

Gunter cleared his throat. 'You boys want to borrow old clothes from me to pass yourselves off as prospectors after gold or silver or something?'

'That's about the size of things, old timer. How about givin' us your help in this matter? It would have to be kept secret, of course, but you wouldn't have any need to concern yourself.'

Dune sounded quite matter of fact and incapable of double dealing.

'If you really wanted to look like prospectors you'd have to have mules with you.'

Gunter's suggestion made Brand wince, but the latter blinked hard, massaged his lush facial hair and rapidly got round to the idea of accepting the offer.

Brand said: 'You'd really lend us your

mules, if we left our horses with you as a gesture of good faith?'

This was Dune's time to look surprised. He knew that Brand was far from happy when separated from his regular mount. Dune, however, went along with the suggestion and when the old man enthused over the simple transaction there was a lot of loud laughter in the cabin.

Gunter went out of doors and returned with a crude wooden ladder which he set against the end log of the loft. 'Better let me go first to test it, boys, on account of some of the rungs ain't all that safe.'

Muttering to himself, the veteran prospector went aloft and before he had been there more than a minute he began to toss down old garments which he had long since discarded. His efforts filled the lower quarters with dust but his visitors were in a good mood and so they did not grumble although they sneezed a lot.

The ladder slipped sideways as Tex

came down, but Brand was agile enough to catch it and to help break the veteran's fall.

'They could all do with a run through on soap an' water, I'll readily admit, but after that they'll suit you, all right. Don't you agree?'

There was not much difference between the partners in size or in weight, but some of the garments fitted them more easily than others.

'You need to look more unwashed,' Tex advised. 'Headgear is important, too. If you have a crumpled hat on, nobody will give you a second glance.'

He looked from one to the other, wondering if they would give him any sort of idea of what they were contemplating, but neither reacted in any positive way, and when the visitors finally mounted to the loft his earlier impression of their potential ruthlessness had returned to him with sufficient impact to disturb his usually dreamless sleep.

11

Being thorough-going professionals, Brand and Dune made nothing of getting up at an early hour and flogging their riding mules hard so as to reach Conchas Creek before a lot of people had roused themselves for the day.

Leaving the two riding animals and the more difficult pack animal tethered to a post just short of the main street, the two partners split up and went their separate ways to do some private observing. A whole half-hour went by before Brand noticed Dune squatting on the edge of a sidewalk not far from the building which bore the name of Bonnie Manton's stepfather.

Written across the woodwork above two separate glass windows were the words, *Harte Jonas Enterprises. Proprietor: Harte Jonas*. It looked exactly like a one-man show which was an apt description for the kind of enterprise Jonas liked to embark upon.

Brand read the words, nodded to his partner and then started to laugh. For a moment or two, the older man did not think of the reason for the levity but when the bearded guitar player lifted his straw steeple hat and scratched his head Dune relaxed.

The ancient borrowed clothes had completely transformed them. Dune, for instance, had on an old buckskin tunic and trousers of the same material. His headgear was a round, undented black stetson with the brim rolled down all the way round.

Brand's steeple hat might once have graced the head of a down-and-out Mexican. It seemed to go along with his faded blue shirt, his tatty bolero jacket and patched denims. Even their boots had been exchanged for older ones which were really far from comfortable. Only their weapons had not been tampered with. At this early stage in their plans they could still laugh about appearances.

'I ain't all that sure that this — this Harte Jonas will take any notice of us in this gear. Besides, I'm beginnin' to feel lousy. So when are we goin' to make a move?'

'If you want to make a lot of money, amigo, you have to suffer a little discomfort. So be patient. We go across to that saloon back there with the tables put out on the broad gallery. It's close enough for us to watch Jonas's place, an' maybe he'll come along here for liquid refreshment.'

Brand murmured his agreement. Slowly, they rose to their feet and dusted themselves down. Dune had the canvas sack of stones tucked under his arm and he was anxious to be in a position to display its contents, if and when the time presented itself.

They found a table which Brand dusted off with his bolero. Service was slow to arrive, but a few blunt remarks from Dune in a guttural voice evoked a response and a small stocky waiter with a bald head came and took their order for two beers.

This liquid nourishment was almost half consumed when a somewhat flashily dressed man smoking a cigar began to approach the Jonas business premises. Dune kicked Brand under the table and the latter half turned in his seat to get a better look.

The new arrival was, in fact, Harte Jonas. Moreover, he had a loud voice and he enjoyed being acknowledged in the street. A brief study showed him to be a weighty man in his middle fifties with a flattened Roman nose and tufted black brows. He breathed rather noisily on account of the difficulty with his nose. On his short upper lip he wore a close-trimmed moustache. Close-set brown eyes and a cleft chin gave his puffy face a homely look which no amount of expensive grooming could alter.

His cream side-rolled stetson had been carefully put on at a rakish angle. The lowest button of the grey waistcoat was left undone, and the dark cutaway coat which fitted over it gave the impression that it had never been worn before.

Jonas cut short a noisy talk with a man across the street on account of his breathing and the need to keep sucking on the cigar. He stepped to the door of the building which bore his name, unlocked it, stepped through and immediately came out again. His tongue was going over his lips and he was staring at the gallery where the two 'prospectors' were taking their beer.

'He's thirsty an' he's comin' this way, so let's get into our act at once.'

Dune kept his voice down because the bald waiter was back in the area again, anticipating the arrival of the big shot.

'You comin' along to join us, Mr. Jonas?' he piped.

The florid man answered in the affirmative and at the same time Dune leisurely took the canvas sack from under his arm and laid it on the table.

166

Steps creaked as the financier stepped up to the gallery and slumped into a chair at the next table to the partners. Jonas glanced at them, decided that they were of no interest, and pulled off his big hat. He suffered from frontal baldness.

'The usual, Mac. Coffee first an' then whisky. You know how I like it, don't you?'

Jonas yawned and slowly mopped his brow, while Brand urgently ordered two more beers before the waiter had gone out of earshot.

Dune began in a loud voice. 'Round about here the banks will surely advance money on silver or gold, but I don't know how they'll react to diamonds, an' that's for sure.'

He emphasised the word 'diamonds' and Jonas's hearing was sufficiently acute to take in the utterance without difficulty. The bulky man shifted suddenly in his chair, although he tried to give the impression that his move was merely due to discomfort.

'Let me see some, will you, Jim?'

This was Roger Brand, in his new identity of Andy Blue speaking out to his friend, buddy and partner, Jimmy Reb. Dune muttered something to show his impatience, shrugged and finally condescended to open the neck of the bag and spill out a few stones. Brand leaned towards him, his hands ready to catch a stone which looked as if it might roll on the floor, but he did it in such a way that he did not hide everything from the covetous fellow at the other table.

'Is it true these blue ones are called sapphires, Jim?'

'I reckon so, Andy, but the bankers would know better. We can be sure they're precious, even if we don't know their technical names.'

They took delivery of their second round of beers after Jonas had received his coffee and whisky, and the waiter's opinion of them went up quite steeply when he caught sight of the dozen or so brightly coloured stones now gracing the table top.

Brand chuckled. 'I've been findin' out things since we left the field. Unknown to you an' all! These here red stones, they're called rubies. Now, Jimmy Reb, confess to me that you didn't know they were rubies! You didn't know, ain't that so?'

'Andy Blue, if you don't keep your voice down I'm goin' to have to do something to make you shut up. You're talkin' about untold wealth in the sort of tones a schoolboy might use. We might be overheard, so shut up an' drink your beer, why don't you?'

Brand appeared crestfallen. He applied himself to the beer as his partner had suggested and when he spoke again his approach was altogether different.

'You think we'll have trouble gettin' the banks to advance enough dollars for us to equip ourselves an' get back to develop the field, Jim?'

'I ain't at all confident the bankers of this town will agree to give us as much as we need. I want a few thousand this time, an' these territorial bankers are mighty careful, so I've heard. Besides, they don't know us an' that's a fact. Why would they want to advance us good United States dinero? Will you tell me that?'

'Why don't you look on the bright side of things jest for once, pardner, an' maybe something will turn up,' Brand suggested.

'Shucks, I don't feel all that confident, Andy. An' what's more those three pesky mules of ours have been out of sight for longer than I'd care to say. Why don't you go collect them, otherwise the only equipment we have will be stolen from us while we're talkin'.'

Behind Dune, Jonas had lurched to his feet. Brand also stood up and he gave the flashily-dressed man a searching look, which made Dune look the same way.

'Good day to you, gents,' Jonas began nasally.

Dune nodded in reply. 'Go on, Andy,

get about your business. I won't be lonely. I'll be talkin' to this here gent while you're away. Don't be long, though.'

Still showing his doubts, Andy Blue moved off up the street, having emptied his second glass of beer. Jimmy Reb moved all his gear over to the table which Jonas had been drinking at and at once gave the impression that the beer had mellowed him. Jonas offered him a whisky and he took it, swishing it around the bottom of his beer glass.

'I couldn't help overhearin' your earlier talk, friend, an' I believe that if you had a genuine bag of diamonds the bankers of this town wouldn't hesitate to advance you money to further your work. Bankers are businessmen, as you already know. But me, I'm a businessman, too, an' I'd like to finance your future operations, if you wouldn't object.'

Dune immediately cooled off. 'Me an' my pardner, we've worked hard for years. Our discovery is ours, every penny it realises. We don't ever want to sell our interests an' that's all I have to say about the matter, Mr. er — '

'Harte Jonas, friend, but you misunderstand me. I wasn't figurin' to buy you out. I simply thought it might help you if you had a man in town like me who could advance a few thousand dollars to help you along. I could buy that sack of stones, if you wanted me to, an' I still wouldn't be out of funds if you needed more for kit and equipment. Do I make myself clear?'

Dune breathed out and calmed down quite obviously. He asked permission to continue the discussion off the street and was escorted quite readily by his new-found friend who took along with him a bottle of whisky to help with the bargaining.

The bawling of a mule some ten minutes later warned Dune that his partner was back on the scene and he stepped out of doors to meet the returning Brand. Securing the three mules took a couple of minutes.

'All's goin' very well, Roger. Almost too well.'

Brand gave one of the mules a vicious nudge with his knee. 'Yes, I suppose so, Clan. What I don't like is what lies ahead of us. Ridin' out into those bad lands an' maybe bein' followed by that dude!' He stepped even closer and whispered. 'Why don't we jest eliminate him in town, take what he has to offer an' clear out?'

Dune shook his head quite decidedly. 'Maybe it wouldn't be wise. Bonnie gave the impression she didn't want us to dispose of anyone in a hurry in this neck of the woods. I reckon we ought to play it the way she suggested. Why ain't you enjoyin' the play-actin'? It makes a change, don't it? All right, don't bother to tell me, you can't stand the clothes. Come on in an' talk nicely to the fat old boy who married Bonnie's mother.'

In the cool interior of the office, Jonas was reclining and trying to appear completely at ease in a big padded chair. He indicated a chair for Brand

and presently all three of them were seated.

'I take it your buddy won't raise any objections to my terms, now that he's here?'

Dune grinned and shook his head. 'I don't rightly think so, Mr. Jonas, he's so keen to get back to those diggings he don't really want to be here at all. Andy, Mr. Jonas here has offered to buy our bag of stones for two thousand dollars, provided we deal exclusively with him an' keep the matter to ourselves.'

'But we need — '

Brand started to protest, but Dune cut him short with a brusque gesture. 'In addition to that, he's prepared to advance us another three thousand dollars for supplies an' equipment, an' we accept his offer 'cause he's promised not to make any talk about tryin' to buy us out.'

Brand stayed thoughtful for a while, and Jonas's cigar plumed smoke towards the ceiling. 'What will he want for the extra three thousand dollars, Jim?'

'He hasn't rightly said, but I reckon we can find him another bag of stones for his money, probably bigger than before. He'll be happy about that, I'm sure. You can hear it from his own lips.'

'Sure, sure, boys. I only want to help, not interfere with your plans to grow rich. I wonder, though, if you'd care to tell me whereabouts your diggin' is like to be. If you didn't happen to make it back again, why, I'd be in a funny position an' that's for sure.'

Brand pointed a finger at Dune and blurted, 'You swore you'd never tell anybody that, an' you ain't goin' to break your oath now! Remember?'

Dune rose from his chair, leaned across the table and patted his irate partner on the shoulder. 'All right, all right, so don't upset yourself. I said that in the days before we made the acquaintance of Mr. Jonas, here. Things are changed now, Andy. All the same, you're a smart boy to want to stay cagey. Let's go freshen up now, an' give Mr. Jonas time to rustle up our funds. He can keep the stones in his safe. They'll not attract any attention if they're under lock and key, will they?'

Brand went on playing his part, always agreeing with reluctance because of the advice of his partner. Jonas almost blurted out that he had enough dollars in his safe in the back room to pay out all the money which had been mentioned, but some fleeting thought of caution made him desist and agree to a further meeting in an hour.

The two bogus prospectors cleared out in good spirits. Jonas covertly watched them go out of sight up the street and then lit his lamp over the desk. For upwards of ten minutes, he ran his hands through the impressive heap of earthy stones, and all the time he was busy his conviction that he was onto the biggest opportunity of his life grew in his thoughts.

None of the three was altogether at ease. While the bogus prospectors were freshening up and eating they were on the lookout for anyone who could see through their disguise and tie them in with earlier episodes in their lives. As for Harte Jonas, although he had a bag of stones in his safe and money which had to be paid out to them, he feared that they might not return. Greed was uppermost in his mind. He was thoroughly hooked on the notion of owning all or part of a diamond field.

The hour's waiting time dragged and the two prospectors seemed to be a long time getting down the street. Eventually, however, they arrived and there were no differences of opinion. Clancy Dune, playing the part of Jim Reb for all he was worth, accepted five thousand dollars in notes and cash and actually signed a receipt for it, using his assumed name. There was a lot of hand shaking before the parting on this occasion and the prospectors gave an undertaking to be in touch briefly once again just prior to their departure from town.

Jonas sighed as they went out of sight with their obstreperous trio of animals, and he had to reopen his safe all over again to gloat over his stones and to reassure himself that it had not been a dream. Some time later he locked up the office and began to wander about the streets.

12

That same morning, Sandy Crease awoke at a late hour and at once decided to sleep a little longer. It was around nine in the morning that he finally roused himself out of bed and took a walk up and down the floor and a look out of the window.

He could see a lot of movement down the street, but nothing he saw put him in an optimistic frame of mind. He felt that Bonnie Manton had duped him in drawing him away from the line cabin and that he might have made personal contact with the men he sought, but for her intervention.

For a time, the imminent danger he would have faced at the cabin escaped him. All he could think of was another setback; another prolonging of the search; less positive progress to report to his employer back in Drovers' Halt.

Presently he dressed and shaved. He paused only long enough to smoke a home-rolled cigarette and then he went off to the telegraph office and wrote out his message. So that his business would not acquire unwanted publicity he wrote it in rather ambiguous words and made out that he was on the lookout for two stolen horses. He felt sure that Senator Hickstead would get the true gist of the message and that he would expect a further progress report from the vicinity of Conchas Creek in the not too distant future.

Having sent the message and chatted with the clerk for a while, Sandy made a brief tour of the main streets looking for familiar faces. Fifteen minutes went by without result and that, he felt, was time enough to work without benefit of breakfast.

By the time he gave his order, the café early morning trade was on the decline. The owner, a tall Greek who also manned the counter, had plenty of time to talk, having eaten his own food before the establishment opened. Sandy smoked a cigarette with him and drew him into conversation.

After talking about this and that, matters of no consequence, Sandy brought the conversation round to the Box M ranch and Bonnie Manton. 'Tell me, Nikki, is there anyone in town who is related to Miss Bonnie? I mean has she any relations in town, other than those on the spread?'

The café proprietor toyed with his thin bristling moustache and looked him over again, wondering what his special interest was. Sandy talked about being a native of Drovers' Halt and knowing Bonnie there and by the time he had run on for a while, the Greek had made up his mind.

'There's a man in this town, name of Harte Jonas. He is an' he is not related to Bonnie. This fellow, you see, married her mother after Rick Manton, the founder of the ranch, died. Jonas has a hold on Box M funds, so they say. He has quite a lot of dollars out of the yearly profits, an' he doesn't work for them.

'So you see, he ain't popular on the spread. An' if you're seekin' to get in touch with Bonnie, as I believe you to be, you'll have to try some other way because she hates him, you see.'

The proprietor ran on for a while longer. Sandy listened well. He enquired about Harte Jonas, what he looked like and where he could be found and then paid his bill, thanking his informant profusely.

★   ★   ★

Harte Jonas went off the street and assumed an alcoholic haze which kept his thoughts from turning up anything good until well into the afternoon. At that time, his unbounded curiosity about the two men who had sold him the diamonds made him do a tour of the main thoroughfares of the town in a tacit search for them.

He had a beer here and a beer there

and adopted the habit of asking questions of loafers and idlers and youngsters with nothing special to do. It was a teenage youngster who informed him that two down-at-heel men with three mules had left town for the south at around three o'clock.

As Jimmy Reb had more or less promised to come along and say farewell before finally riding out of town on the return journey to the diamond field, Jonas did not attach any credence to the boy's story and it was not until early evening that he began to think that, after all, the two men who had quit town might be his partners.

Their failure to make further contact filled his mind with new doubts and anxious speculation. He was so disturbed that he took a long cold bath to enliven himself and return to his office once more to look at his stones. This time, he pocketed about half a dozen of them so that he could fondle them as he walked about the town.

On the gallery of his favourite saloon,

Jonas drank a good deal more whisky. He imbibed steadily, his eyes taking in the comings and goings of his fellow men, in case his contacts of that morning were still in town and looking for him.

No one remotely like either of them showed and after a time merely fondling stones in the depth of his pocket gave the acquisitive man no further satisfaction. He called for a lamp, although there was still plenty of daylight, and under the pretence of reading a paper by its extra light, he produced his stones and rolled them this way and that being careful not to spill them off the newspaper. So intent was he on this little game that he completely failed to notice a tall, blue-eyed young man with a lot of sandy hair poking out from under a sweat-stained flat-crowned grey stetson.

Sandy Crease, the observer in question, stood in the roadway not many feet away from the man he now knew to be Harte Jonas. He had his back turned to the saloon and its wealthy patron. In that fashion, he gave no indication of his special interest.

★ ★ ★

Jonas gave a gasp as a sudden noise further up the street made him jump and squeeze the paper. All but one of the stones he was juggling with stayed in the wrapping, but the other one bounced down the length of the table and dropped into the loose dirt surface of the street.

Sandy, who was very much on the alert and keen to know what Jonas had been doing, was quick enough to notice the progress of the stone. In a flash, he had put his boot sole over it. No one noticed his move. Jonas bellowed for help, his nasal tones carrying easily into the saloon proper. The waiter who usually served him came into the open, picked up the lamp and peered around the floor with it.

Two strangers from another table,

who had been half asleep, joined in the search in a half-hearted manner in case there was a reward in the offing. Sandy waited until the uproar had more or less died down and the search had been called off. He watched Jonas sink several fingers of whisky and then he bent down. Under the pretext of cleaning dirt off his boot toe, he slipped the stone into the palm of his hand and hoped he did not look too suspicious.

The actual contact of the hard stone with his palm gave Sandy a thrill of excitement. Could there be a connection between this stone which seemed to be precious and the haul which the killers had made in distant Drovers' Halt?

If not, it was a coincidence that stones should come into his investigations again. After all, the west was rich in gold and silver and copper, but fields of precious stones were almost unheard of. And yet the dropping of a single stone by a man connected with Bonnie did not necessarily have to mean anything. Maybe it was his imagination working over again; wishful thinking, or something of the sort.

Still, a few questions were in order, after the contact.

Sandy seated himself quite deliberately opposite Jonas, and the latter prompty reacted in a rebellious sort of way. He was about to suggest that there was plenty of room for strangers up against the bar when Sandy held out his hand and opened it, revealing the stone which nestled there.

At once, Jonas's expression and attitude changed. He called for an extra glass and poured whisky for Sandy, who then saw his opportunity for further enlightenment.

'You're Mr. Jonas, I believe, an' I'm quite sure you have a genuine interest in precious stones. Me, I have that same interest, but not because I want to possess them. I'm chasin' a couple of hard-eyed killers who murdered the brother of a senator back in Drovers' Halt and robbed him of a sack of stones which he was takin' to a cutter.

'Now, it jest happens that I've traced these two hombres right along to your town, Mr. Jonas, an' as I'm taking money from Senator Hickstead of Trinidad, Colorado, you'll allow I have every reason to be interested in anyone else in this town toyin' with precious stones.

'Could I ask you if you by any chance bought those stones you have from men in town today?'

The question was a sudden one, closely followed up by a lot of words calculated to put the half-inebriated financier in an anxious frame of mind.

Jonas swallowed hard. He had trouble with the butt end of his cigar for a time. With an effort, however, he recovered his poise and his mind partially cleared. 'Why sure, I didn't intend to tell anyone, but I did buy these stones today. Only the men I did the deal with weren't any hard-eyed killers. They were jest a couple of tough prospectors from the

— the place where they'd mined them.

'There wasn't any question of passin' on stolen property. Why, right now they're either on their way back to the mine, or buyin' stores ready for pullin' out.'

Jonas was working hard to convince his listener. He was listening to himself, too, and having griping doubts from time to time, mostly based on the fact that his partners had not found time to come back and wish him farewell.

Sandy paused for a few seconds and then made a suggestion. 'Mr. Jonas, I did you a little favour jest now. I wonder if you'd allow me to have a brief look at your pardners, supposin' they're still in town. If they're genuine an' like you say they are, ordinary prospectors, nobody has anything to bother about. Least of all yourself.

'It's jest that I have to satisfy myself, my client bein' an important figure in the west an' him wantin' results for his money.'

Jonas attempted a blustering laugh, but he dried up rather quickly.

'My boys wouldn't hesitate to sell their stolen property at a big profit to the first sucker who came along,' Sandy added, as though talking to himself.

His words further troubled his listener but a little more time had to elapse before the frightened financier was prepared to co-operate.

'What did you say your name was, mister?'

'Sandy Crease of Drovers' Halt. Son of the mayor an' brother of the town marshal, for what it's worth!'

'But you ain't a peace officer yourself, are you, Sandy?'

The latter grinned, taking a little of the heat out of the situation. 'Nope. I'm no peace officer. I wanted to be, but my brother an' the good folks of Drovers' Halt didn't see it my way. All I'm interested in is runnin' down two killers, an' maybe recoverin' some stolen semi-precious stones. So, what were you goin' to say?'

'I was goin' to say that I might jest try an' give you the chance to look over my pardners, jest to be on the right side. So why don't you tell me where you're stayin' in case I have to get in touch with you in a hurry?'

Sandy gave the name of the hotel and his room number. He then left his new contact and openly walked away into another street. As soon as he was out of sight, however, he backtracked and attempted to keep an eye on Jonas's movements. This he was successful in doing, but nothing came of it.

No one remotely like a prospector came looking for Harte Jonas and the worried financier became more and more restless until around ten o'clock when it became obvious by his action that he intended to make his way to the hotel and contact Sandy.

The latter hurried to his room well ahead of the other and composed himself without his boots upon his single bed

Jonas knocked the door gently five

minutes later. He was admitted without delay and offered the one good chair in the room, a creaking wickerwork seat of doubtful vintage.

'Can we talk now, Sandy? Will anyone overhear us?'

Sandy closed the window, checked everywhere and assured his visitor that they could not be overheard. 'What's happened, Mr. Jonas?'

'Nothing. Nothing at all. My contacts, the prospectors, must have pulled out without sayin' a farewell. That doesn't have to mean they ain't what they claimed to be, but what you were sayin' earlier, that troubled me. I mean if they're sellin' stolen property they ain't likely to be on their way to dig up more stones, are they?

'An' if they *do* have a field of stones an' they aren't honest, I'm out of pocket by several thousand dollars. No man wants to be taken for that sort of a fool.'

Sandy nodded. 'So what is it you want to do, Mr. Jonas?'

'I'd like to have you with me when I ride after them, Sandy. What do you say to that?'

The young investigator was about to point out that they would not know which direction to take, but Jonas was chuckling for a change and fumbling about in the pocket of his coat. Obviously, he had some sort of a lead.

13

Jonas left the wicker chair, crossed to the bed and squatted on the end of it, waving a piece of paper in his hand which was about eight inches square.

'If I show you this, Sandy, I have to be certain you'll keep it a secret. How about that?'

'I won't be spreadin' your business all over town, Mr. Jonas. Now, what is it you have there? Some sort of map, wouldn't you say?'

The older man showed immediate disappointment when Sandy made his guess. Nevertheless, he was still very interested in what he had to show. Sandy fetched the hanging lamp and between them they got a really good look at the paper. On one side of it was a receipt for money signed by one James Reb. The date was for that day. On the back of it was a pencilled map, the source of Jonas's excitement.

'I don't think this fellow, Jim Reb, meant to leave me with a map showin' the way to his diamond field, but he was full of good liquor when I last saw him and he must have used his little map to make out my receipt for money! I reckon he won't know what he's done with it. Does the name Buckeye's Folly mean anything to you?'

Sandy decided that this was the name of some local landmark, but he had to confess to having no knowledge of it. Jonas chuckled throatily and nudged him in the side with a sharp elbow.

'Most folks round about here do, though, amigo. It's a narrow windin' valley to the south-east of town. Some hombre called Buckeye once thought he'd found gold in it, but all he had when he got to the assayer's office was some rock or coal or something with a telltale streak of yellow through it. So they call the place Buckeye's Folly!'

At that hour in the evening, Sandy's patience was not at its best. He prompted: 'An' Buckeye's Folly is where the two prospectors are supposed to have gone?'

Jonas made an effort to pull himself together. 'Not exactly, but Buckeye's Folly is the route to this spot in the Bad Lands, Triple Canyon. That's where the field is supposed to be, an' that's where I want to go with you sidin' me, if you have sufficient interest.'

This time, Sandy supposed, was a good time to make Jonas think a whole lot more. He wondered how best to make him see that his deal of the morning might very well go sour on him.

'I suppose you realise they may not have ridden that way at all, Mr. Jonas. That map may have been given to you on purpose to take you out of town for a while, an' nothin' more.'

Jonas gave out with a noise compounded of a cry and a groan. He actually rose from the bed and turned on the spot before sitting down again and turning his small beady eyes to

Sandy. The latter returned the lamp to its hanging holder and then flopped on his bed once again.

'How long is it since you sat a horse on a protracted ride?' young Crease wanted to know.

Jonas started to bluster, but the stony look in his companion's blue eyes cut him short. The bulky man looked this way and that, and finally admitted that he was out of condition.

'When you ask that question does it mean you'll give it a try? My route to Triple Canyon an' all?'

'We could give it a try, as soon as I've assured myself that your contacts have really left town. After all, it's possible they're sleepin' off an overdose of beer somewhere after bein' in the Bad Lands for too long.'

Sandy talked on and as he did so, Jonas became calmer and more relaxed. He was rocking on the bed when the young investigator's words unsettled him again.

'In the event that your prospectors

are my killers, I might have to shoot them on sight to prevent them from gettin' away from me. You'll have to get used to that idea, Mr. Jonas. Whatever sort of a workin' arrangement we have between us my first loyalty will always be towards Senator Hickstead. That must be understood.'

This consideration made the older man blink. He crossed to the window and opened it several inches. He seemed to have forgotten how keen he had been earlier not to let anyone overhear their topic of conversation. Before he said any more, he produced a cigar and lighted it. In an effort to cement the agreement between them, he handed over another and offered the tip of his own for lighting purposes.

'But in the event they happened to be headin' for that place on the map I'd have to ask you to hold your fire for a while. Do you think you could accommodate me in that way? After all, there might be something in it for you if they led us to the diamond field, even if they were wanted for a killin'.'

'If you have the map, why should you bother about havin' the prospectors ridin' ahead of you?'

'Because there might be snags on the way we don't know about. I'd feel more confident if they were up in front. Now, what do you say?'

Sandy's mind went back over the events since Dune and Brand had almost sent him to his death off the side of that ridge near home. He felt certain that he had almost run into them at the line cabin on Box M territory, and now he had the chance of following them up again, providing he was on the track of the right pair.

He asked about their appearance but Jonas was not very good at describing people. Not even those he connected in his mind with a fortune. As he was getting nowhere, Sandy decided to try himself. He gave out detail after detail about the fellow who called himself Dune without getting anywhere.

It was when he started to describe

Brand's closely-trimmed down-turning brown moustache and beard that he began to get a positive reaction. Jonas was nodding without showing a lot of confidence. Feeling that he was on the right track, young Crease got off the bed and began to pace the room.

'The fellow with the beard had long restless fingers. Did you ever see a guitar?'

He paused in his striding and Jonas automatically started to shake his head. This time he changed his mind quite suddenly and began to nod.

'There was a guitar. I remember it now. It was on the back of one of those grey mules they had outside the office. Does that mean you really do know my prospectors?'

'Nothing is certain,' Sandy admitted, but he looked pleased in a rather grim sort of way. 'An' you're still waitin' for an answer to that earlier question about whether I would refrain from shootin' them before they reached the diamond field.'

Jonas perked up again, thinking that Sandy had come to a decision about his question, but such was not the case. The younger man started to peel off his shirt, prior to going to bed. All he would say about the unanswered question was that he would give his verdict later.

★　★　★

Over breakfast, Sandy tentatively gave his agreement to the question of holding his fire before anyone arrived at the diamond field. All the time he was eating, he was turning over in his mind all the imponderables, all the things they could not possibly know about before the event.

What if one of his earlier theories was right, that there was nothing at all to be discovered at the nether end of Triple Canyon? The more he thought the more morose he became, and he forbade Jonas to discuss the matter any more.

All through the forenoon, and subsequently the afternoon the young investigator combed the town for signs of the elusive renegades. He had no joy at all and nothing happened to justify his protracted search until late in the evening when he had come to the conclusion that he had lost his sense of proportion.

He was seated with Harte Jonas in front of the latter's favourite saloon, smoking yet another cigar and slowly drinking tepid beer when a peculiar uproar started to permeate the street. Piping above the sounds of voices was a simple musical instrument of some sort which later proved to be a tin whistle.

Some fifteen or twenty men looking for some sort of diversion followed the whistler, keeping step to the Confederate marching tune he was playing. Jonas stood up to see what it was all about. He grinned to one or two of the townsmen, but the man actually playing the tune had little interest for him. The financier sat down again, but Sandy leaned over the rail and had a closer look as the marching group went by.

'Who's the fluter, Mr. Jonas?'

'Oh, some ex-prospector from out in the country. Name of Tex Gunter. Owns a shack in a remote valley not far from the Box M spread. He only shows up about every three months or so. I wonder what brought him this time?'

Jonas asked his question but there was no real curiosity apparent in his manner. Sandy, on the other hand, was immediately interested when he heard mention of the Box M ranch. Emptying his beer glass, he excused himself and went down the street after the noisy group.

The music ended abruptly. Gunter had come to a stop in a wide open space between two buildings and there he put together a few old packing cases in order to light a fire and have his food heated over it. Several of his old cronies squatted on the ground while Gunter knelt down and coaxed the fire to go with his long grey beard tucked into his red and green shirt for safety. The old man was breathless through fanning the reluctant flames with his hat by the time Sandy had taken a place at the back of the crowd.

'You're in funds, Tex, an' no mistake,' a man in a derby remarked. 'How did you manage it this time?'

Gunter nodded and chuckled. He set up two sets of forked sticks and put another one across the top of them with a plucked chicken skewered along its length. He had collected the fowl for his food on the way into town.

'Had me a bit of luck the other day, Nevada. Two hombres called on me. Like a fairy tale it was, in a way. They exchanged their good trail clothes for some old stock I should have thrown out ages ago. An' that was not all!'

Gunter gave his chicken a couple of turns and his mouth watered.

'An' what else did they give you, you old son of a cougar?'

'Well, I was breakin' in my third mule at the time, a vicious red-eyed beast it was with a couple of deadly hind hooves. I was sweatin' it out, gettin' him used to havin' panniers on his back when along they came. They had with them a couple of fine ridin' horses, but they was so keen to become real prospectors that they borrowed my three mules and left their horses behind!'

'So why didn't you come ridin' into town on a fine upstandin' horse, Tex?'

The man who answered to Nevada was still doing the quizzing, but several of the other hangers-on were equally keen to hear the explanation. Sandy listened as carefully as anyone. He could think of two men who might have wanted to borrow mules.

'Because doggone it they came back again. Same pair of fellows. Still wearin' the old clothes I'd used from way back for prospectin' in. I thought they'd want their proper trail gear back an' their horses, but such was not the case.

'First thing I heard when they got to talkin' about their latest needs was that they wanted to keep the mules for a much longer trip. So they suggested buyin' them this time. I listened an' I agreed because I figured they were keen enough to pay a good price. Which they did. And so that's why I'm here in town, with my pockets full of dinero! Yippee!'

'Quit soundin' off with the yippee noises, Tex, an' explain about the horses! Why didn't you come in on horseback?'

'Because my business acquaintances took away their horses, as well. Didn't I explain that?'

Nevada laughed. Others joined in. One or two yawned and wondered if there would be more food, other than the chicken which Tex was capable of eating all by himself.

'How much did they pay you for the mule?' an unidentified voice queried.

Gunter laughed and turned in the general direction of the questioner.

'Enough! Enough, I tell you, but it wasn't all in money, though! I could show you things that would make you envious of me. Maybe I will, at that. Hand me that enamel plate, amigo.'

Someone pushed the plate into his eager hands and everyone eased forward to know what he had to show them. Very slowly and carefully he unbuttoned his shirt and spilled out into the plate a handful of small hard objects. They were round in shape and in three different colours.

Chuckling easily to himself, Gunter gently gyrated the plate and had the stones running round inside it. There was considerable uproar from the onlookers. Some said that he was fooling them all, that he had a child's marbles along with him, but others who had not imbibed so much were clearly impressed.

'You don't mean to say your prospectors were after diamonds in this part of the world, do you, Tex?'

'I'm not tryin' to tell you anything at all, friend, but I can say this. I didn't grumble when they offered to pay part of what they owed me in precious stones!'

There was a general rush forward. For a time, the food was forgotten as Gunter displayed his stones. He was willing to show them to almost anybody, so long as they did not insist on handling them in that indistinct light.

Sandy stood back and contemplated the scene. He had thought at first to ask questions of his own, but Gunter had revealed so much that he felt sure that they were his elusive pair of killers, Dune and Brand.

Jonas met him along the street. 'All right, Mr. Jonas, we set out for Triple Canyon tomorrow morning. I believe your business acquaintances are likely to make the trip to the diamond field an' they could be already on their way. Are you still as keen as ever?'

'Ain't nothing at all likely to put me off, young fellow. Nothing at all.'

Jonas wanted to get ready that same night, but he allowed himself to be dissuaded.

14

Jonas knew where Sandy wanted to eat and the breakfast which the proprietor of Jonas Enterprises ordered amounted approximately to a mixed grill. Young Crease, who had awakened in a tense frame of mind, found himself somewhat relaxed by a contemplation of his partner's eating habits.

Jonas ate as though he was consuming his last meal. Before the food was properly finished no fewer than two merchants came into the café and politely whispered queries into the older man's ear.

He answered briefly and soon put them right. Clearly, they were preparing an order for food to be consumed 'between towns.'

At the smoking stage, there was a short discussion about the need for a pack horse. To Sandy's surprise, Jonas declined to take one along. He answered with the manner of someone who is keeping something back and Sandy did not take the trouble to probe further in the matter.

A half-hour later, they left town, heading towards the south-east at a brisk pace. Jonas was mounted up on a broad-barrelled buckskin, a chunky sort of horse which had plenty of bottom. During that first punishing day, the older man sat his saddle well and did not complain although it was clear that his bones were aching and his muscles giving him a lot of trouble.

During the first night out in the open, Jonas slept badly. He muttered a lot when he ought to have been asleep and his face looked strained as breakfast was prepared. During the scratch meal, they talked a lot about their present position relative to Buckeye's Folly, Triple Canyon and the riders they were following.

'I think we ought to have sighted

them before now, Sandy. After all we've been ridin' down a regular trail all day, an' they could scarcely have gone in the right direction if they hadn't taken the same route!'

Sandy patted the irate fellow on the back. 'You want it all to happen in a day, Mr. Jonas. If there's untold riches ahead of us no doubt you'll get your deserts, but it'll take time. An' don't forget those two riders didn't start out from Conchas Creek like we did. Their startin' point was a veteran's shack several miles nearer the route. So we ain't likely to catch them up much before Buckeye's Folly. If you think about it, you'll see I'm right.'

Jonas approved of Sandy's reasoning before they mounted up to start the second day's travel. 'Do you still think the boys we're followin' are your two killers?' he wanted to know.

'I'm practically certain of it, pardner. But that shouldn't worry you at this stage. We go off the beaten track this mornin'. Don' be afraid to nod off in the saddle now and again, if you feel like it. I'll be sure to keep watch.'

* * *

During that day there was little conversation. Sandy kept himself to himself and tried to weigh up the future and what it held in store for him. In summing up his own capabilities, he had to remind himself that he was little more than a back street Indian fighter when it came to using firearms.

Back in Drovers' Halt he had popped away at bottles and similar targets, but if he had to blaze away at Dune or Brand he might just be found wanting. Harte Jonas had weapons with him and he looked capable of using them, but Sandy had his doubts about the man with the strangle hold on the Box M ranch. His brain might be very keen when there was money in the offing, but out here in the wilderness with a couple of cold-blooded killers ahead

Harte Jonas might be out of his own league.

Twice during that day Sandy saw obvious sign. He connected it up in his mind with horses accompanied by mules. The smaller plates of the crossbred animals showed up very clearly among the marks left by the others.

The second night out in the open was spent in camp just short of the tortuous valley known as Buckeye's Folly. On this occasion, Jonas slept quite well and he was the first awake the following morning. Due to his determination, the pair were ready to ride again within two hours of dawn and this progress led to the first sighting of the bunch they were following.

Some few hundred yards into the valley Sandy caught sight of smoke which came from a fire used to prepare breakfast on.

'We're catchin' up, Sandy! Why don't we creep up real close an' take a look at them while they're still thinkin' about food?'

'I don't think that would be wise, Harte,' Sandy returned soberly. 'What I propose is to move over to one side and take a look at them through the glass from a high rock. You want to come along with me, or are you content to ease off a little and smoke?'

Jonas was so keen to go along to the lookout spot that he made it appear as though his partner was not trustworthy on his own. Five minutes later, Sandy led the scramble up hill and came out first on a flat rock which afforded a good view. He was so hot with the climb, however, that his eye misted up the nearer of the two lenses and he had to wipe it off and start again.

By the time Jonas toiled up behind him, he had the group in focus and he was the first to be surprised by the numbers. There were not two figures taking food down there but three! By dint of careful observation Sandy thought that he could pick out the two men whose trail he had followed since Drovers' Halt, but the third person, a long lean figure in a black steeple hat and a red poncho mystified him.

He was whistling almost soundlessly to himself when Jonas gripped his elbow and insisted on taking over the glass. The financier reacted in a similar fashion.

'Hey, what do you make of that? Those two boys never said anything about a third partner! Why did they keep it back from me, I wonder? Do you have any ideas on the subject? Have you come across that Mexican in your travels?'

'If I have I don't recognise him,' Sandy murmured. 'Somehow I don't think he's a Mexican, though. His skin is too fair for a full-blooded Mex. Maybe the fellow is wearin' that outfit as a disguise the same as the other two.'

'You still think they're pullin' the wool over my eyes, Sandy?'

'I do, indeed, Mr. Jonas. The end of this journey is jest about the most unpredictable thing that's ever happened to either of us. Don't build up on anything. That's my advice. Before very long you may have to use those weapons you brought along with you.

'Do you have any known enemies who might especially want you dead?'

Stunned by the suddenness of the question, Jonas managed a blustering laugh, but his partner knew there was no real mirth behind it and soon he became silent again.

'Are you serious?' he asked, staring hard.

'Of course I am. Out here, in the country, you can't afford to be too cagey with the only ally you can count on in miles. Well, have you?'

Jonas licked his dry lips. 'Well, there's a couple of folks over at the Box M ranch got no reason to like me much. In fact, I'd go so far as to say they hate me. But that ain't the same as arranging to have me killed or anything like that. Do you really think we're up against that much?'

'Anything might happen. Me, I'm prepared to shoot to kill, too. I warned you about that soon after we met. Don't go along with the idea that you're bein' introduced to the pot of gold at the end of the rainbow by two nice young fellows who want you to have it all.'

'You mean three nice young fellows, don't you?' Jonas argued.

Sandy nodded. The discussion ended rather lamely and they were soon backtracking to their horses and taking a breather to allow the other party to make a start. During most of that day there was little conversation. The nerves of the second pair, if anything, were a little more on edge.

Buckeye's Folly was a geographical location of some scenic beauty but the eyes of the beholders were not brightened by it. The valley floor which was strewn with the rocks containing the yellow markings was simply a route to another place. A place of reckoning for five people with a ruthless streak.

* ★ * ★ * ★ *

The first group of riders camped a few yards inside the most easterly of the three canyon mouths. This was the one by which the second group were supposed to enter. A dotted line on the map which Jonas had acquired pointed the way up the canyon towards a point in the west side cliff. Closely drawn dots suggested that there might be a way through that cliff into the middle canyon. The close dots then indicated a similar access to the third canyon and the supposed field of precious stones was located well up the third canyon on a point near the east cliff.

As the light faded, Brand played his guitar but the other two were usually looking away from the fire and watchful of their pursuers rather than mindful of the music.

Sandy and Jonas, who were travelling lighter, came to within a few hundred yards of the first camp. They noted where the fire had been lighted and at once back-tracked until they were over a mile away. Now that the canyon mouths were yawning at them in the early hours of darkness they had no intention of giving their enemies a chance to jump them.

That night, the pursuers took it in turns to sleep for two hours and in that way they managed to get through the night undisturbed and feeling moderately safe. In the morning, it was Sandy who made the breakfast while Jonas smoked and talked.

'Sandy,' he began, 'we both looked at the map long enough to know what is drawn on it by heart. I'm reasonably satisfied that trouble lies ahead of me. Those two boys haven't spent a lot of my money on equipment like they said they would an' they've taken on another man I'm not familiar with. If there is any wealth along there at the spot they marked out for me, I might have to fight for it. Clearly, you also think I'm in some danger, so I'm tellin' you right now before we enter the canyons that I want us to split. I want you to go one way an' leave me to do the direct follow-up as the map indicates.

'That way through from one canyon to another may be a stream bed or something of the sort. In any case, I feel confident that I can find my way alone an' that's the way I want it.'

'I know I promised not to try and arrest or shoot those two young renegades before we reached the site of the field, but what do you expect me to do if you're ambushed?'

Jonas shook his head this way and that. He sniffled through his flattened nose and finally came up with an answer. 'If I'm gunned down, I know you'll feel free to act accordin' to your conscience, Sandy. I wish you luck, an' if I seem a little distracted before we part, don't think anything of it. I'll be on the move jest as soon as I think *they* are.'

★　★　★

At the same time as the pursuers were making plans, a parallel discussion was taking place between the other three. The figure in the black steeple hat was very busy with the breakfast, more so than on any other morning. This activity was a clear indication to Dune and Brand that their other partner, Bonnie Manton, was about to make some change in their plans.

Bonnie finished her meal first. 'Boys, I'm real glad you came all this way on my say-so. It was good of you. I asked you to lure my stepfather into this remote neck of the woods because I wanted him out of the way. I wanted him robbed of his ill-gotten gains and I wanted him dead. I couldn't say that to a lot of men, but you are the kind who understand.

'Now that we're so close to the spot where we indicated the stones were, I'd like to ask you to go on and show an interest right where they are supposed to be. You might even sprinkle one or two more there for the finding.

221

'I wouldn't ask you to do this if there was no way through the canyon. Folks think there ain't no way through the third canyon, but they're wrong. You can't get all the way through usin' the ordinary mouth because there's been a big fall of rimrock halfway down an' that blocks the way, but if you go through those linkin' tunnels from the other canyons you come out beyond the fall an' that makes it straightforward to go right through.'

Clancy Dune toyed with a small cigar. 'Bonnie, you wouldn't be sayin' all this if you didn't intend to break away from us. We'll do as you say, an' we'll keep on goin' through. When are you plannin' on leavin' us?'

Roger Brand echoed the same question. The girl gave each of them a rather wan smile. 'Almost right away. I shall enter this complex of canyons by the middle mouth. Don't have any fears for me, boys. It's been nice knowin' you. We won't do any embracin' in case someone has a glass trained on us. So this is it, the time of partin' . . . '

Within minutes, Bonnie's white stallion was saddled up and ready to be ridden. On this occasion, however, she took it by the head and led it out of the canyon, skirting the cliff-like west side of the entrance until the high ground receded and gave way to the next opening. As soon as she was out of sight, Dune poured the coffee dregs on the fire and made hasty preparations to move on.

While they were still busy, Brand had a question to ask. 'There was a time when that girl bothered me, Clan. That was in case she preferred you to me. But I'll say this for her, she was our type of girl. Judgin' by the way she's been actin' recently, I'd say she really hates that old hombre who's been following us. Do you think she wants to be on hand to see him die?'

'I'll say she does,' Dune confirmed. 'Not only that, she wants to despatch him herself! How does that strike you?'

'I believe you're right,' murmured the bearded guitar player.

He cinched up, whistled briefly and swung himself up into the saddle.

15

Slowly the shadows lifted in the deep floors of the three canyons. Bonnie Manton had started out first and she had moved into the middle canyon without being observed by the two pursuers. Shortly after that, Dune and Brand mounted and started up the canyon in which they had camped. Sandy and Harte Jonas were both ready at the same time, but the older man rode off alone in the wake of the killers.

Soon, Jonas reached the other camp. He paused long enough to study it, but he learned nothing that he had not known previously and he shrugged impatiently and started forward again.

Left on his own with his mission not completed, young Crease felt as if he did not belong. He was a long way from his base and about to enter the sort of country which normally attracted law-breakers and undesirables. All he could be sure of was that three of those who were ahead of him were capable of murder without conscience, and he was not in any position to be critical of them because he was committed to shoot to kill if that form of self-defence became necessary.

One mystery which he would have liked to clear up before entering upon the last stages of this struggle was concerning the identity of the third man in the first party. He felt certain that it was not anyone known to him, and that he had to assume that the third party was also a killer. It would not do, at this stage, to underestimate anyone at all.

Sandy yawned. Provided that he kept clear of Jonas, he had a free hand. He wondered how he could use his present freedom to further his own ends. The only possibility he could think of was to gain altitude and try to observe the other riders from a new angle. Further conjecture almost put him off. He thought that by the time he had reached sufficient height on one of the cliff walls those in front might have penetrated so far as to be out of sight. His restlessness prompted him to do the climb and he did so at the expense of his boot heels and only just in time. His chest was still heaving when he pulled out the spyglass and pointed it up the east-side canyon.

The group furthest advanced was making a turn as well as putting up a lot of dust. He brought them as sharply into focus as he could manage and attempted to count them. The three mules were dancing about at the back and through them he could only see two mounted riding horses.

At that time of the morning his first reaction was that he had counted wrongly or not seen clearly. Seconds later, that party rode out of sight and all he had to look at on that side was Harte Jonas who was cautiously following up with his full body hunched forward on the back of the plodding buckskin.

Sandy looked downwards from his perch and decided at once that he did not like the sensation of height. In conniving to find an easier way down again he manouevred himself into a position where he could see quite a way into the middle canyon.

In order to rest rather than for any other reason, he used his glass again and received the biggest surprise of the morning to date. Clearly marked along the canyon floor from the mouth was a trail of horse shoes. Whoever had left the first party had gone right up the canyon bottom, steadily weaving through rock which had fallen countless years earlier. And spreading above the trail was a light curtain of dust, the top surface of which was curiously enlightened by the probing rays of the sun.

As soon as he saw the new prints, Sandy's brain began to work. He discarded the theory that the lone rider had gone up there to be permanently away from the others. He felt sure that anyone going up the middle canyon would encounter again those travelling up that on the east side.

He had made up his mind which route he was going to take long before he was back at floor level. The sun appeared to have strengthened during his climb and now that he had something new, something positive to attempt, his spirits rose.

After the briefest of halts, he turned his skewbald in the new direction and presently picked up the tracks of the rider who had gone ahead. That made three riders in one canyon and two in another. How the inevitable clashes would turn out, however, was still a matter of guesswork.

* * *

All three canyons were quite extensive in length. Towards midday the riders in the east-side ravine were still making progress. The sun was slowly crossing the heavens, but because the canyon was narrowing they had the impression that they were going deeper and heading into almost immediate night.

Harte Jonas, his wits sharpened by danger and the outside possibility of untold wealth to be won, fought against any inclination to get too close to the others. In the past, the prospect of gain had prompted him to cut a few sharp corners, but he had never killed for gain. At this stage, however, he was prepared to use his weapons whatever the outcome.

As the valley floor darkened he moved even slower, relying upon his ears to keep him out of immediate danger and using his knowledge of the pencilled map to keep his interest alive.

Gradually, the leaders drew nearer to the spot where a divergence had to be made. Close under the cliff on the inward side, Dune and Brand were reduced to slow probing of the wall. Every fault had to be studied from close up in the search for an opening.

About thirty minutes went by with

no success. After some discussion, they pegged out the mules and backtracked. Dune stayed close to the wall while Brand moved away from it. The latter was the one who found the shallow groove in the soil where a stream had meandered along many years earlier.

Since the waterway had dried up, much rimrock had fallen in the area obscuring the route and many minutes were lost before the mules were recovered and pointed in the right direction. From ten yards away, the cleft did not appear to be negotiable.

The partners dismounted and peered into the opening. The dank coldness of the place and the bats which flew out of it made it anything but pleasant and each regarded the other in a special way which suggested that alternative arrangements might be made.

'What if there's a fall in there which we can't see until we reach it,' Brand pondered unhappily.

Dune shrugged. 'Either we go in with a burnin' brand or we dig ourselves in here and do what has to be done at this spot. Me, I'm inclined to chance takin' the tunnel. I think it would be a kind of poetic justice if that character, Jonas, died right at the spot where he thought the diamond field was located.'

Brand was still thinking that his partner's thoughts were clouded by his feelings for Bonnie Manton, but he did not air his views.

'All right,' he approved, 'if you feel that way about it, we'll give it a go. In any case, Jonas will soon be off our backs, won't he?'

'Either tonight or tomorrow, I guess,' Dune returned, with a dry chuckle.

In the event that the brands did not burn well in the damp air, they took one each and went to some trouble to ensure that they were properly alight and burning easily. After that, the mules played up. This latest problem was solved by having a rider at the rear of them.

Although the going underfoot was soft and sandy in places, there were no difficult pitfalls. Twenty minutes later, they were out in the comparative daylight of the middle canyon. Five minutes ensured that they were still very much alone. They took a drink, rubbed down the horses and at once moved across the floor of the canyon in search of a similar opening on the far side.

From time to time, the bright blue heavens above them made them look up. A great turkey buzzard glided across the sky, making the utmost use of its broad wing-spread. Brand's gelding side-footed to avoid a rock and that brought the rider's thoughts back to more immediate problems.

In order to get into the third canyon, two rocks of small size which weighed heavily had to be shifted by mule power. This caused a delay and tired the two men whose energy was quickly sapped in the peculiar air encountered at great depth.

As soon as the way was clear, Roger Brand, who was feeling the strain, pushed his gelding into the lead, leaving Dune to follow up with the rest of the animals. This second tunnel was negotiated in slightly less time and the third canyon had the benefit of more natural light which made them feel a little better.

The dampness of the atmosphere made the guitar player cough. He was annoyed as well because his fragile instrument had brushed against the side of the tunnel and some of the varnish had been scraped off it.

He said abruptly: 'Have you thought of where we're goin' when we get out of this canyon, Clan?'

'Sure enough, Rog. We come quite soon to the Canadian River. If we follow that waterway we shall cross the Texas border. I can't see anyone followin' us that far on account of our recent doings, can you?'

Brand shrugged and declined to argue further. After a short rest, they moved on again, marvelling at the bird life and the small animals which abounded in such a remote place. A slow journey of an hour took them to the obvious spot for the diamond field. There was a place directly under the cliff on the inner side where a considerable fall had taken place.

This particular location was slightly different from others of its kind because several tons of soil had come down from above. The portion of terrain under observation resembled a huge rockery with only the tops of rocks sticking out from it here and there. Fast growing ferns and other green plants had sprouted on the top of it and camouflaged it to some extent.

'This is where we camp, an' that's where we plant our few remainin' stones,' Dunne decided finally.

'So let's get ourselves a meal before Jonas arrives on the scene,' Brand remarked morosely.

Overhead, the sky already seemed to be darkening. The time was merely mid-afternoon, but the sun had travelled so far towards the west that the lessening daylight made it seem much later. Neither of the partners had had any previous experience of such a phenomenon.

Soon, a fire was going and its flames produced a blossoming halo of light which improved their outlook and their spirits. They ate well, drank a lot of coffee and finished off with a few fingers of whisky.

With the passing hours, tension returned to them. The shadows appeared to hem them in. It was a difficult atmosphere in which to try and relax, let alone sleep. The restlessness of the mules added to their discomfort and neither could say anything to comfort the other.

'I wonder how Bonnie's makin' out,' Dune muttered, as he rolled his blanket more tightly around him.

'Unless she has nerves of iron she'll be sufferin' the same as we are,' Brand commented.

Another fifteen minutes of restless tossing and listening convinced both of them that it would be as well to be doing something. Dune had the idea of planting the stones and then finishing off the whisky. Brand offered no argument to the suggestion. Upwards of a score of diamonds, sapphires and rubies were pushed lightly into the surface of the fallen earth. For extra measure, Dune scattered another dozen without bothering to bury them.

'What now?' Brand queried, when the job was done.

'We have to assume that if anyone approaches us it means trouble,' Dune surmised. 'That bein' so, we make up our bedrolls but don't stay in them. We take our weapons an' move away to rock shelter. Agreed?'

'Agreed.'

All the time they were making up the dummy rolls they were glancing up-canyon into the gloom. No one appeared to be close, although occasionally they heard small sounds which might not have been made by the canyon's natural population.

The rocks they chose were low-lying

ones which would give adequate protection provided that they stayed in a prone position. This seemed reasonable until the damp started to come through their clothing. After that, they were twitching and rolling to keep warm . . .

★   ★   ★

The nearest human to the killers' position was the man from whom they had most to fear. Sheer determination had drawn Jonas along in their wake. He had negotiated the first tunnel without benefit of light, relying on the instincts of his horse to make the somewhat perilous through journey.

Unknown to him, Bonnie Manton had been within fifty yards of him as he crossed the middle canyon but as she had not planned for him to die in that neck of the woods he negotiated the second tunnel without ever being aware of her. When the time came to emerge from it, he cunningly left behind his horse and only took along with him his canteen, weapons and a spyglass.

The slow, cautious walk up the third canyon accounted for a lot of his energy, but he kept going and by the time true night showed in the form of stars far above, he was within gunshot distance of the two men writhing about near the 'field'.

After a time, he became aware that there were no bodies in the bedrolls and that was all the excuse he needed to assume treachery. Subsequently, he was caution itself. He moved further along, giving the camp area a wide berth, and positioned himself upon a big flat rock which gave him a height advantage of six feet or more over the other two.

Jonas rested for five minutes to get his breath back and make his simple plans. He then lobbed a stone towards the blaze and waited for the first reaction. It was slow to come, although both Dune and Brand had heard the noise and seen a small shower of sparks.

It was Dune, the older of the two, who finally put up his head and shoulders for a better look. There was just sufficient eerie light to pinpoint his silhouette. In the confined space, the rifle sounded off like the booming of a cannon. Dune's body jerked, twitched and turned over, having absorbed the first bullet through his neck.

Brand gave a cry compounded of disbelief and fear. He panicked just long enough to come to his knees and turn around. Again the rifle coughed brief flame and a bullet winged towards him. He suffered a slight shoulder wound which made it difficult for him to take proper cover. Two further shots missed him, but the fourth aimed at him entered his chest after ricochetting off the side of a rock.

Brand went down writhing and twitching in a way which no man could have faked. When at last he lay still, the whole area round about the scene of the action assumed a deathly silence.

Jonas had to work to control his nerves for upwards of ten minutes before he could get down from his vantage point and approach the scene of his handiwork. A first scrutiny of the two victims showed that they were both well and truly dead, but his jumpiness made him fetch a burning stick from the fire and look them both over again.

Having finally assured himself that he had nothing further to fear from them, he returned to the fire, helped himself to some of their coffee which had not been consumed, and then went looking for stones.

In the gloom, the actual place of the planting was not so obvious, but he was dedicated to what he had to do, and presently he saw one or two stones glowing dully in the light from his torch. He enthused over the few he found, but he was not sufficiently enthralled to believe that he had found a true field.

One stone, in fact, had surfaces cut on it which could only have been done by a worker in precious stones. A lapidary. This discovery ended all the mystery. Except that he had only accounted for two men when there should have been three in the group.

Gaining confidence from his earlier sharp-shooting, he returned to the fire determined to make himself a meal out of the other men's food.

16

A good solid meal had been eaten and Jonas had collected the greater part of five thousand dollars from the clothing of his victims before the next development. In receiving back his money he felt a certain warmth within himself which went some way to restoring his undermined self-confidence. It was one thing to be duped about a faked diamond field, and another to be actually relieved of thousands of dollars.

While his heavy supper was going down, Jonas stalked around the fire and thought about Sandy. For the first time since he had mounted the successful ambush, the young investigator was back in his scheming.

Since they parted there had not been the vaguest suspicion of a contact. What were the chances of a reunion that same night before weariness drove him under the blankets?

Jonas stayed still on the cliff side of the fire, blowing his cheeks and wondering how many of his small cigars were left and still the right shape. He was fumbling them around in the pockets of his buttoned waistcoat when something beyond the fire startled him.

He blinked hard and looked again. He let out his breath in a noisy sigh, already satisfied that his first fears were unfounded. Someone had actually lit a lamp and judging by the position of it it seemed to be quite close to the rock from which he had sprung his ambush.

Stepping carefully, he moved around the fire to the near side. Already he was beginning to think that Sandy was joining him for the night. All around the lamp was the usual eerie glow, but there was no clear sign of the person who had lighted it. Jonas blinked hard and cleared his throat. Bending forward from the hips, he called: 'Hey, Sandy, is that you?'

He thought he heard the sound of someone moving but he was not sure. He had a six-gun at his waist, but his hand was slow to go towards it. Suspicion was slow to be rekindled in his mind.

'*Sandy?*'

The lamp stayed exactly as it had been since he first saw it. There was the sound of movement and something else which sounded like choked off laughter. Jonas shifted his feet. For a fleeting moment his mind turned to other things, such as ghosts. But he dismissed such considerations and instead started to move slowly to one side.

Much nearer to him than the lamp and considerably off to one side he thought he saw a substantial shape on the move. The laughter came again. It came from the spot where he had seen the shape. The laughing welled up in volume and then his hair started to prickle. There was only one place where he had heard that sort of laughter before, and only one person he knew of who laughed like that.

Bonnie! Bonnie Manton . . .

But how could she be mixed up in all this? How could she be in this canyon of death so many miles away from Conchas Creek and the Box M ranch? Jonas groaned in spite of himself. The fear which had been totally absent when he tackled the renegades now came back to him and with greater intensity than he had thought possible.

If Bonnie was in this canyon then she must have planned all that had happened! She had planned his end. His death.

Reason struggled with his fears. The only unknown quantity in the present set-up was the third man in the original party of riders. Could Bonnie have been that third figure all this time? A *girl?*

A woman in a poncho and a big black steeple hat? He was still thinking over this seeming impossibility when the figure loomed up even closer. Even in the darkness the bulky outline of the poncho and the steeple hat were visible, and the figure was coming straight towards him.

Jonas tried to call out, but words failed him. He clutched his throat as though willing the words to come out. A late effort made him pull the revolver out of the holster but he felt he had to speak before he used it. All he could think of to say was the name.

'Bonnie! *Bonnie Manton!*'

His words came out clearly that time. They had the effect of curtailing the advance of the shrouded figure. He was holding his Colt forward with a shaky hand when the tiny flame blossomed adjacent to the ponchoed figure. The other revolver barked and Jonas felt as if he had been kicked in the stomach.

He lurched backwards, his gun arm lowering of its own accord. Other gunshots mingled with the sound of swelling laughter which came and went in another-worldly ethereal fashion.

Another bullet ripped into the upper part of his chest. He was on his way down when a third hit him in the head.

He died with a fleeting mental impression of an angry girl in a ranch house kitchen pointing at him and swearing eternal vengeance and looking as if she meant it. He lay in a still, bulky heap beside the fire which he had shared with two other dead men.

The laughter had died down to a recurring sob by the time Bonnie reached the fallen figure. She turned to the fire, pulled out a big burning twig and used it to examine him more closely. With her half boot toe, she prodded the hated man this way and that.

Presently, she knelt down beside him and went through his pockets. She discovered the bulky amount of money which he had taken from those who had died earlier and transferred it to a pocket inside her poncho. Next, being still in the grip of emotions scarcely controllable, she spat across the corpse.

Her voice trembled as she made her last communication with the hated man. 'I warned you, Harte Jonas, but you wouldn't be warned. You were never a Manton an' you didn't know what you were tanglin' with! Now you've got your deserts, an' serve you darned well right! An' here's a partin' gift from your greatest admirer.'

She stepped a little closer and pointed her gun at the bald skull. Her finger tightened on the trigger. There came a click but that was all. The chambers were empty. For a moment or two she was undecided whether to reload or not. And then she walked away.

She had accomplished her objective, but not without cost. She was almost a complete woman again as she moved towards the other bodies, nibbling nervously at her underlip.

★   ★   ★

Sandy Crease was terribly conscious about having missed out on the time of the action. If it was fate which had kept him from the clash between desperate men, then he did not like it. The last terrible sequence of events had left him with a conscience.

If anything, the second outbreak of shooting had staggered him more than the first. There was a reason for that, but because his mind had boggled it was not for several minutes that he realised quite why it had been so.

When the main reason for his shock became clear to him he was standing somewhere in an isolated position on the floor of the third canyon with his Winchester tucked under one arm. It was the laughter which had so shaken him. Even a furlong away in that atmosphere he had recognised it, and the mingling of the human sounds with the gunshots told him a whole lot more.

There was a great finality about the second lot of shooting which assured him that he could do no good for anyone by proceeding on his self-appointed march up the rest of the canyon straight away. Feeling superfluous in a troubled sort of way, he turned on his heel and retraced his steps to the place where the restless skewbald awaited his return.

All the time he was walking he was thinking about the laughter and what it all meant in relation to the identity of the third person in the poncho and steeple hat. For days, he had thought that Bonnie was back at home on the Box M away from all this trouble. But how wrong he had been! Sandy saw as clearly as Jonas had done that she had to be fully involved with the plan to get rid of Harte Jonas.

And now, unless he had totally misread the signs, the greedy financier had been eliminated. Sandy found himself shaking his head about it, as if a man he had ridden with, eaten with and slept alongside of could not have just died of bullet wounds in this remote part of the territory known as the Bad Lands.

He shook his head some more about

the other consideration; that Bonnie Manton, the girl whose attentions he had almost fought for in a barn dance in his home town half a lifetime ago, that *she* should be up this remote fastness of nature with a smoking pistol in her hand. The same girl he had swum with on her family's ranch.

He sighed as he backtracked and remembered that she had started to deceive him about Dune and Brand on that same afternoon when they had slipped his attentions due to her uninhibited performance as a decoy.

The whinnying of the skewbald drew him to the correct spot and by then he thought he knew what his actions ought to be.

He went over to the horse, a sensitive animal which could easily be spooked in the enclosed atmosphere of the canyon, and rubbed its nose, speaking words of comfort. Next, he prowled around in the dark for firewood. Ten minutes work raised ample kindling for a start. Without hesitation he put a match to the blaze and fanned it with his stetson until it was thoroughly alight.

For several minutes more he threw wood on it, breathing hard all the time and trying to give himself the impression that he was warding off the forces of darkness by his efforts.

This had been a long and taxing day for him. Clearly, the events which had occurred in the last hour or so indicated that he, Sandy Crease, was probably the least skilled of the quintette who had ridden into the canyons in the everyday western business of finding a route not adequately marked.

All had gone well in the early hours. He had tracked the person in the poncho without any difficulty. Now, with events seen differently in retrospect, it seemed that the pseudo-Mexican had known that he was doing a tailing job.

Bonnie must have deliberately lured him further up the middle canyon than she had ever intended to go. Before the other three, Dune and Brand, closely followed by Harte Jonas, had entered the middle section via the tunnel, Bonnie and Sandy must have crossed the line between the cliff tunnels and gone on well past them.

Bonnie's cautious progress had been slow, but not slow enough to allow Sandy to relax in his vigilance. The upper reaches of the middle canyon had been every bit as dark by early afternoon as the two on either side.

During the hours of the afternoon, the quick-witted girl had taken her chance to double back down the other side of the canyon and slip away through the tunnel which led into this, the third canyon.

Because he had not negotiated the first tunnel, Sandy found the mouth of the second tunnel only after a pro-tracted search and when an extra couple of hours had elapsed. To make matters more complicated an owl had spooked the skewbald in the middle of the tunnel and a sudden side-step had thrown him into the wall and rendered him unseated.

Although he was shaken he had retained hold of the reins. The rest of the way into the open was accomplished by him on foot.

Here, in the middle of canyon number three, he felt altogether alone and quite dispirited. He felt like a mature man who has no illusions left to shatter. In the middle of all his dissatisfaction was this one remarkable girl, Bonnie Manton. Bonnie Manton, dancer, shop-keeper, carver of wood and rancher's daughter. He could have added other descriptive words, but his mind shrank from using them. He found himself looking up-canyon and shuddering.

He looked up at the stars and found some comfort in doing so. They were there to be stared at, even if they confirmed man's insignificance. They were the same stars shining over distant Drovers' Halt and all the people who looked upon the town as home, and that had to mean something to a lonely young man driven to maturing too quickly.

Gradually his mind started to function again. He built up his fire to fine proportions and moved around it, checking on the rocks and vegetation. On the up-canyon side there was a fallen tree with a couple of gnarled branches groping upwards.

Almost opposite was a tall rock some four feet or more in height. Some built-in instinct made him lay his bedroll down between the rock and the fire. His saddle went under the end nearer to the rock, and he surrendered his weathered grey stetson to complete the tableau.

Unknown to him, a similar ruse had been attempted unsuccessfully further down the canyon. Nevertheless, such a move was new in Sandy's experience and he felt that it might just keep him out of trouble. He had heard things which led him to believe that the opposition might be very tricky.

As a last finishing touch, he laid down his Winchester beside the plumped-up roll and tossed his spurs to one side of it.

* * *

When she came, Bonnie came openly, putting down her feet firmly so that anyone who was awake would be fully aware of her approach. She had the lamp with her and she swung it by her side. From time to time she hummed a sad song. At every step the floppy steeple hat kept bobbing as if working to the same rhythm. Fifty yards away, she called out.

'Hey, is that a private camp or can anyone join?'

Her voice sounded as alive, as youthful and as attractive as Sandy had always remembered. He wasted a few seconds before answering, wondering if his own voice would betray some of his doubts about the coming encounter.

'Come on right in, amigo. Take the weight off your legs an' warm yourself, why don't you?'

Bonnie slowed a little. The poncho was held tightly around her body with the hand holding the lamp sticking out from under it. She came to a halt quite close to one of the upstanding branches of the fallen tree. She was looking straight towards the bedroll and smiling.

'I know who you are, amigo.'

Sandy blinked unseen. He was kneeling tensely behind his rock. 'I never made any secret of my identity, amigo.'

Bonnie giggled and moved around the projecting branch. She lowered the lamp to the ground a little to one side of her and appeared to be nearly exhausted. Her shoulders slumped and she pulled off the steeple hat which had so effectively helped to disguise her for so long.

'I know a lot of fellows who would be up out of their bedroll an' round this fire to make me welcome in a more obvious way.'

'Maybe some of them don't have the power of movement any more, Bonnie. There's a thought now.'

The girl gasped. She reached up and began to pull out the pins which had held back her shoulder length hair for so long. One by one she tossed them to the flames. Finally she shook her head and all her tresses swung loosely about her neck and shoulders. She sighed.

'Sandy, don't you find it lonely in this God-forsaken place? Back there is the end of the world. Those three men, they've eliminated one another. Clan Dune, Roger Brand an' my old step daddy, Harte Jonas. All dead.'

'You must feel satisfied, nevertheless, Bonnie. After all, you wanted Jonas dead an' you accomplished it. I would never have believed you could do it with your own hand if you hadn't laughed at the time.'

The cold appeared to be affecting the girl. Her arms disappeared under the poncho. She seemed to hug herself.

'Was it so bad to want to be rid of a man who had battened on to our ranch? A man who was suckin' it dry through his greed?'

'Whatever he had done, you shouldn't have killed him. You murdered him with your own hand. You *know* what you did. I believe you came here fully prepared to do it.'

The girl's reaction was very sudden. The poncho billowed out as the Colt revolver, fired from underneath it, started to pump bullets at the bedroll. The hat flew, the saddle jumped. The blanket was jerked aside. Chunks of rock flew from the front of the protecting finger of stone.

Sandy counted until all six bullets had been fired. He then stood up and hurled the dagger which had killed Mark Hickstead in the direction of the seated girl. It landed where he had intended it to land, quivering in the soft timber of the fallen tree, two feet from Bonnie. The shock of its landing brought her back to the present and her predicament like nothing else could have done.

Sandy stepped clear of his protective rock, swinging his revolver.

'I'm goin' along to the other camp fire now, Bonnie. Those dead men hold no fears for me. I'll bury them in the mornin'. In case you're hopin' to come out of all this with honour, don't bother to plead.

'I know the depths to which you will plunge to get your own way. You won't work any more successful ambushes on this trip. Tomorrow mornin' I advise you to start the return journey at an early hour. As soon as I've finished my diggin' an' the writing of a detailed report I shall be on my way to Conchas Creek.

'There, I shall tell them all I know about the happenings in this canyon. Stay long enough to tell your brother that Jonas is dead, an' then start ridin' again. If you get out fast the local authorities might not search for too long, seein' as how you're a woman an' Jonas was unpopular in town.'

He collected his horse and came over to her again. 'You understand what I've been sayin', Bonnie?'

She nodded without looking in his direction.

'All right, then. There's one other spot in this county which won't welcome your company any more. I refer to the town of Drovers' Halt, of course. *My* town. *Adios*.'

If she answered he did not hear her.

The still figures near the other fire had no terrors for him.

He finally settled in for the night with an adequacy of blankets not far from the form of Harte Jonas. For a long time, the twinkling of the stars fascinated him, and then, inevitably, his eyelids grew heavy.

He slipped towards a dreamless sleep guarded by the dead. His last remembered thoughts of that night gave him a strange serenity. Jacob S. Hickstead, he felt sure, would approve of his conduct of Hickstead affairs.

Others in the town, his kin possibly, might be more critical of his behaviour on the difficult assignment, but he felt sure that the days when they laughed at him were gone forever.

THE END

We do hope that you have enjoyed reading this large print book.

Did you know that all of our titles are available for purchase?

We publish a wide range of high quality large print books including:
**Romances, Mysteries, Classics
General Fiction
Non Fiction and Westerns**

Special interest titles available in large print are:
**The Little Oxford Dictionary
Music Book, Song Book
Hymn Book, Service Book**

Also available from us courtesy of Oxford University Press:
**Young Readers' Dictionary
(large print edition)
Young Readers' Thesaurus
(large print edition)**

For further information or a free brochure, please contact us at:
**Ulverscroft Large Print Books Ltd.,
The Green, Bradgate Road, Anstey,
Leicester, LE7 7FU, England.
Tel:** (00 44) **0116 236 4325
Fax:** (00 44) **0116 234 0205**

MIDNIGHT LYNCHING

Terry Murphy

When Ruby Malone's husband is lynched by a sheriff's posse, Wells Fargo investigator Asa Harker goes after the beautiful widow expecting her to lead him to the vast sum of money stolen from his company. But Ruby has gone on the outlaw trail with the handsome, young Ben Whitman. Worse still, Harker finds he must deal with a crooked sheriff. Without help, it looks as if he will not only fail to recover the stolen money but also lose his life into the bargain.

BRAZOS STATION

Clayton Nash

Caleb Brett liked his job as deputy sheriff and being betrothed to the sheriff's daughter, Rose. What he didn't like was the thought of the sheriff moving in with them once they were married. But capturing the infamous outlaw Gil Bannerman offered a way out because there was plenty of reward money. Then came Brett's big mistake — he lost Bannerman and was framed. Now everything he treasured was lost. Did he have a chance in hell of fighting his way back?